Dude, Where's My Fox?

by Kyell Gold

DUDE, WHERE'S MY FOX?

Published by FurPlanet
Dallas, Texas
http://www.furplanet.com

ISBN 978-1-61450-197-8
Printed in the United States of America
First trade paperback edition: September 2014
Cover and all interior art by BlackTeagan
"Permanent Market" title font by Font Diner, *http://www.fontdiner.com*

For Fuzzwolf and Teiran
who know where their foxes are

CONTENTS

CHAPTER ONE

It wasn't like Steven to just leave me alone after sex. Usually we cuddled for a bit before washing up. But I was definitely naked on the couch with a pleasant, slippery ache under my tail where he'd left his passion, and a pleasant, sticky mess on my stomach where I'd lain in the results of mine, feeling better than I'd felt in weeks. Months, even. Steven had really grabbed me, pounded himself into me, and had enjoyed himself a lot—as had I, both of us moaning and panting and generally making way more noise than usual. I'd been pent up for a while, but still. Even now I was left with a nice floaty feeling, like the whole thing had been a dream.

Actually, I didn't remember Steven leaving. I sort of remembered him saying into my ear that he loved me, but unlike the lingering pleasure in my groin and under my tail, that memory fluxed as I focused on it. He'd said it to my eyes, our noses touching, not slumped over my back. Hadn't he? And we'd been in our bed when he'd said it, whereas now I was…leaning against the back of a couch, but the smell was wrong. Had we gotten a new couch? Why was my memory so fuzzy?

I imagined myself saying, *Hey, Steven, you fucked me silly*, and that brought a giggle up from my gut. I must have passed out or something, and Steven went to clean up, or to get himself some water. I shifted my head to look at the half-open window.

The room spun and lurched with a familiar and not entirely welcome precariousness. Whoa. Okay, I was drunk.

God dammit. Waking up was supposed to be a clean start, not continuing a drunken night. And not even the best part of a drunken night.

Clearly, from the smell under my tail, the best part was behind me. I hadn't been asleep for long, because the lube was still tacky, if not slippery, and it was still dark outside. Maybe it was the next night and I'd slept the whole day? Could I still be drunk a day later?

I guess I could cross 'having sex while full-on drunk' off the purity tests from now on. Must have had a whole bottle of wine.

No, not wine. My muzzle tasted sour and fruity. Mixed drinks? Since when did we make mixed drinks? I rubbed the bridge of my nose against soft leather.

Leather? This wasn't the couch in our Freestone apartment, because we didn't have a nice red leather one, and also the people downstairs didn't play…I cocked my ears. What were they playing? It sounded like tropical island music, but sped up. And there were a lot of people talking.

A party. Steven and I had gone to a party. And had sex in an upstairs bedroom? That wasn't like us at all. I'd had fantasies…but Steven would never really do it. I blinked and looked around the room, nose up to catch the scents. Lube and jizz, first off, and then leather and something else in the air. I sniffed, scanning the plain brown carpet, dark brown wood, red wallpaper and paintings that I couldn't quite make out. None of them had any smell stronger than the thick smells of leather and sex. But through the partly open window, flowery smells drifted in to me.

Shit, that was right. It was April and I was at…someone's spring party. Someone with a big mansion, someone named Mc-Something. And he lived out on…

The cool breeze smelled of the ocean, which was right, but it wasn't the same ocean. Less fish, more garbage. I breathed in again, and memory clicked into place. It smelled different because…because I wasn't even in Freestone. I was on Great Island off Port City. But Steven hated Port City. Derek had brought me here, not Steven. That meant that the warmth under my tail…

Hadn't been left there by Steven.

Fear seized me and clarity crackled through my head. I'd cheated on him? My heart pounded, the floaty drunk feeling spinning into nausea. Who the fuck had…well, fucked me, then? I lay there inhaling the scent of mostly my own come, and replaying the scattered memories in my now far less drunk head.

His arms had gripped me around the chest, black fur coming almost all the way up to the elbows, russet fur from there up to his shoulders. His ivory neck ruff had been soft against my muzzle (*like Steven's*) and the weight of his chest had settled between my shoulders. His long red tail had wagged, his frisky white tip flicking until he slid around behind me, and his black ears had flicked with excitement when I pulled his pants down.

I remembered the feel of his cock in my paw, in my muzzle, and sliding into me, the warm swell of his knot. I remembered grunting and huffing, mine and his, and the feeling of soaring together, of being connected to him by more than just his cock, and his paw on me, working, stroking. I remembered the two of us coming, shuddering, collapsing into the cushions together. I remembered his soft bite on my furry ear.

I remembered everything except his name.

For a wolf, name isn't the main thing. We go by name, but also by scent and by look, by body language and fur. And I'm pretty good at that kind of thing, only less so when I'm drunk. So I had kind of a vague picture of a fox, a little taller than me, with bright amber eyes—or were they brown? A pretty pink shirt—or maybe it was salmon? No, it was cornflower. I remember thinking Steven had a shirt just like it.

He smelled enough like Steven to confuse my drunk nose, too. In fact, his scent was—

I curled myself around and stuck my nose behind my balls. The movement made my head swim and the room spun and tilted on an axis somewhere in my chest. I put out a paw to steady myself. Fuck. Apparently my body was still drunk even if shock had cleared my head. Yeah, now I remembered getting some fruit-flavored drink and gulping it down, someone big—Derek—propelling me toward a guy, me putting down the drink and picking up another one, and I vaguely thought that when I'd bumped into the fox, that second one had not been the one I was holding.

When the room stabilized enough that the smells didn't make me queasy, I braced myself and inhaled. The lube smelled strong, and over it I could smell fox musk. Not too strong, and there was a light smell of latex. Good. At least he'd used a condom. But I kind of remembered him pushing his dripping cock into my fur before putting the condom on and actually sticking it in me.

Inside me. Someone other than Steven had been *inside* me. My ears flushed and flattened against my head. And I'd enjoyed it, too. How could I enjoy it? How could I just let some random guy take my clothes off, grab my cock, fuck me, without thinking about how it would make Steven feel? I'd never betrayed him.

But it had been the first in a long time. That only made it worse; I'd held out for that long and then just gotten drunk at a party and fallen into bed—er, couch—with the first guy to come along? Who had this guy been, anyway? And more importantly, what was I going to tell Steven?

I looked around for my phone. Derek would be able to tell me why I was in this room with this couch, why I was in this mansion with dubstep luau music playing, and why Steven was—

The last piece of my memory slapped me across the muzzle, so hard I squeezed my eyes shut. Steven was in Freestone. He was in Freestone and I was in Port City because we weren't together anymore. The memory of him saying he loved me was from last year; he hadn't said anything like that to me since the week before Valentine's Day, when he'd said, *Lonnie, I still love you, so this is really hard for me to say. I met someone...*

The guilt of having slept with someone else surged into the shame of being dumped, experienced all over again thanks to the tricks of memory and alcohol. Somehow, I managed to be both ashamed of myself for not being good enough for Steven and ashamed of myself for sleeping with someone else.

But maybe it hadn't been someone else. Maybe it had been Steven. He could've come down in secret, seen Derek's ScentBook update, waited until I was drunk. If he hadn't told Cranston, if he wanted it to be anonymous, if he missed me...

Again, I curled around to sniff below my tail. The scent was exotic, exciting, intimate, and it wasn't Steven's. I lingered there a little too long, and felt a stirring in my sheath.

Part of me didn't feel guilty, at least. Weirdly, getting aroused again, a completely visceral response, helped calm down my thoughts. Even if I didn't belong in this place, reeking of sex with some anonymous fox, I certainly didn't belong to Steven anymore either.

Memories of making love with Steven had gotten me through a bunch of lonely nights, and there were certain things I would focus in on: the shape of his cock in my paw, the way he knew how to jerk me off after three years of practice, the easy way he slid into me, the little twist of his hips when he was pulling his knot out. But now the memories were confused with my mystery fox. I couldn't remember him pulling his knot out; he must've done that while I was passed out. But he'd sort of fumbled around my shaft; he'd rubbed around the little pudge on my waist and seemed to like it.

All right. My heart had slowed, the drunk was mostly wearing off, and if the hot flush of cheating guilt hadn't completely cooled, at least it wasn't incapacitating. Logically, the first thing I needed to do was get my clothes on and get out of the room. Then I could find Derek, and after that I could process whatever emotional baggage this had left me with. So I straightened out while keeping my balance, alert for any disorientation. The room behaved itself as I stretched out and saw my t-shirt and underwear on the plain brown carpet. Slowly, I slid off the red leather cushion, knelt, and picked them up.

There wasn't a bathroom connected to this room. I tried to remember if we'd passed one on our drunken search for a vacant room. Problem was, most of what I remembered of the search was his paw in my pants, squeezing my hard shaft, sliding around to draw claws under my tail, while I wriggled and stumbled forward, my paw wrapped around his shaft, the two of us pulling each other along and laughing. About what? I sort of remembered, through an alcoholic haze, a movie discussion…a comedy I liked?

Maybe it was a sex comedy where the main character ended up naked in a strange house's bedroom and had to figure out how to get out. I sat on the couch, which was already going to require cleaning, so me smearing some lube around wouldn't make much difference, and anyway, the smooth leather felt nice. I didn't want to put on my pants or boxers until I'd cleaned up, but I couldn't clean up until I left the room, and I couldn't leave the room until I put on pants or boxers. My head was starting to hurt the more I thought about it.

Fucking Derek. What the hell was he thinking, bringing me to a party where I didn't know anyone and didn't know where to wash up? *Don't get drunk and fuck in a room without a bathroom*, he'd say.

No, that was something I would say. Derek would say, *just go out in the hall, you fucking ommie. Own it.*

Maybe he—or my semi-drunken approximation of him, complete with derogatory evaluation of my social standing—was right. I eyed the door. The fox, whoever he was, had gotten up and out of there and had either put his pants on over a sticky sheath, or had walked naked out into the hall.

Or…I looked around the room. It was a small study, and the red leather armchair across the corner matched the couch I was currently wagging my tail against. On an end table, between them, were two plastic cups and the bottle of lube we'd used. I thought I remembered Derek pressing it into my paw. *You're gonna get lucky*, he'd said, and I'd told him that was less likely than an earthquake hitting the mansion.

When I focused on the portraits on the walls, I saw foxes, otters, deer, wolves, bears in leather bondage outfits. The dresser held leather straps and collars and a couple ball gags, as well as electric gadgets whose purpose was plain, and others I could only guess at. I felt momentarily bad for just having had plain old vanilla sex. Then I found what I was looking for on the floor behind the couch: a small towel.

It smelled of the same musk that was sticking up the fur behind my balls. I found a dry-ish part of it and wiped back there until it was mostly dry, and then put my boxers and pants on. One last time, I looked

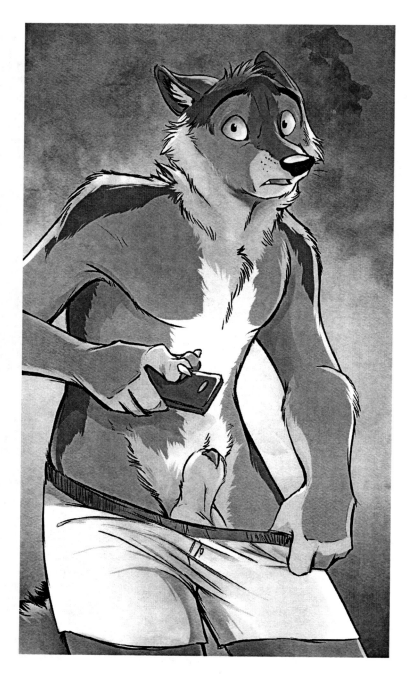

around for any trace of my mysterious lover, but the room did not reveal any more secrets.

I fished my phone out of my pocket to text Derek and found a message from him waiting for me.

Derek: Hey, you passed out somewhere?

Passed out—well, I had been. I should send him a picture of my sticky sheath and balls, I thought. Derek would appreciate it, no doubt; he'd dated a porn star last year and while we were catching up last month, he casually showed me pictures of him and his boyfriend naked, aroused, sucking each other off, fucking. I'd sat sort of frozen because none of my other friends ever did anything like that. The one time I'd timidly brought up maybe videotaping ourselves to Steven, he'd said, "And find the video on the Internet in five years? Are you crazy?"

Just coming down, I typed back, and started for the door.

My paw landed on the couch's armrest to steady myself. In the shine of the room's light, the smears of lube and other stuff on the cushions shone out at me and the smells rose to my nostrils again. I'd done that. Again, in my head, I heard fake-Derek's voice: *Own it, don't be an ommie.*

Well, fine. I dropped my pants and boxers and positioned the phone to get a photo of my sheath.

And that's when the door to the room opened.

I stood there with a phone in front of my naked crotch staring at the tall fox in the blue collared shirt, hanging open to show off the mussed white fur of his chest and stomach. One of his paws rested on the doorknob and the other disappeared behind his back.

"Oh," I said, tail curling back. "There you are."

He stared down at me, nostrils flaring. "Sorry," he said. "Room was quiet. You about done?"

Done? I felt cool air around my balls and set the phone down, hurrying to pull my pants up. "I, uh…"

That's when the rabbit came around from behind him, shirtless, with a flowery lei around his neck and the fox's other black paw down the front of his pants. A little bit of pink showed just over the waistband. "You wanna watch or join, that's cool," he said, and grinned a bucktoothed grin up at the fox.

"Sure," the fox said diffidently as I fastened my pants and grabbed my phone. "Just can't fuck in the hall or McMinaver kicks y'out."

"Nah, I'm done." So this wasn't my mysterious lover. Which made it a lot more embarrassing that I'd just been taking a pic of my junk in front of him. I snatched the dirty towel and hurried out into the hall. "There's lube on the, uh—"

"Got our own," the rabbit giggled as he stumbled past me, the fox's bushy tail curled around his rump. The two of them disappeared into the room and the door slammed with a concussion that put a jump in my step and an arch in my tail as I hurried away.

There was nobody else in the long hallway, and all the doors were closed. From downstairs I could hear talking and music, and as I padded along the carpet sniffing for soap, a jaguar hurried up the stairs toward me. He turned, braced himself against the wall, tail flicking, and then made a hoarse coughing noise, doubled over, and threw up.

I turned away from that charming sight and found the sharp scent of soap in my nostrils. Bathroom, dead ahead, and unlike most of the other rooms on this floor, it was unoccupied. Granted, the jaguar might need it more than I did, but, well, maybe not so much right now.

As I undressed and washed off my family jewels and my back door, I wondered again if the fox I'd bumped into in the hallway had been the one who'd, well, bumped into and inside of me. Had he been so drunk he'd just stumbled down to find another tail to slide under? And then either hadn't recognized me, or hadn't said anything in front of door number two?

I didn't think so. There were a bunch of foxes at the party, probably thirty out of the three hundred guests. The chances were it was another fox, a different fox. I nodded at myself in the mirror as I adjusted the t-shirt. Certainly I didn't feel like *I* had to go off and get fucked again. I wouldn't want to deal with the guilt, for one thing. You're broken up, I told my reflection. You have been for two and a half months.

Funny, that didn't make me feel any better. It wasn't like I was a prize catch; I'd been lucky to be with Steven for three years. If I were all white or all black like one of those movie-star wolves, or a six-foot-four gym regular like Derek, then I'd be getting stuffed with cock left and right.

I cupped my paws under the faucet and lapped up water, then did it again. When I straightened, I rubbed down the reddish-brown fur atop my head, which was sticking up and mussed. The fox must have licked it up between ear-bites.

The black tips of my ears flicked back. The bites had been nice, and had been something Steven had never done. I still couldn't shake the hope in the back of my head that maybe Steven had come down to the party, had seen Derek posting about it maybe and had worried about me. He'd watched me get drunk and then had tried to protect me like he used to. And then…then I would feel a lot better about being nicely warm in back and worked out well in front. Or I could reverse those last two. Either way, if I imagined it was Steven, the guilt receded.

I still had the sticky, messy towel, which I guessed I should leave in the bathroom. I lifted it to my nose first. His musk was still on there, and it was also still on my boxers. What the hell. I pulled them on anyway, then my pants, and brought the towel to my nose one more time. Musky, kind of lightly fruity—although that was probably just the fruity drinks flowing downstairs—and a kind of woodsy scent that I liked. It wasn't Steven, but…

My phone buzzed again. *Derek: Pics or it didn't happen! You go bro!*

Apparently in my haste to put the phone away, I'd sent the picture of my messy crotch to Derek. He didn't quite get modern slang, but he misused it in the most adorable way, and it put me at ease.

I shut the phone off and slid it back into my pocket. I wished I could just find this fox and ask him…not if he wanted to see me again—Derek had warned me about that. But just if I was good.

(And to make sure it wasn't Steven.)

Someone pounded on the door, interrupting my reverie with a slurred string of incoherent words. I hurried to the door and opened it, and the jaguar pushed past me. He stumbled to the sink reeking of vomit and made that hoarse cough again, so I backed out into the hall before I had to watch another round.

Ten minutes of breathing with my head against the wall cleared my thinking a little bit more, and then I felt ready to go meet up with Derek. As I descended the wide marble staircase, I scanned the room. A six-four muscled wolf wasn't hard to spot, and after about fifteen seconds I found Derek talking to a black rat in a red-fringed black lace vest and glittering red sequined pants. They stood a couple feet away from the extravagant island flower sculpture, which had already lost noticeable chunks. I passed a deer chewing on a hibiscus he'd clearly taken from the sculpture, and tapped Derek on the arm.

"Hey, bro!" He wrapped an arm around my shoulder and squeezed, nearly pulling me off balance. "Hey, Jeremy, this is my buddy Lonnie I was telling you about."

The rat wasn't the most extravagantly dressed person I'd seen that night, but he was probably the flamiest one I'd talked to. "Pleasure to meet you." Jeremy's voice matched his outfit, high and fancy. "What have you been getting up to?"

Derek's nostrils flared. "He just got fucked upstairs. Wanna see?"

Blood rushed to my ears as they flattened against my head. I stared at the floor, sure that everyone in the room had heard and turned in my direction. The echo of *you cheated on Steven* rang through my head and my tongue felt two sizes too big for my muzzle. "I, uh."

I was panicking because Derek was actually fumbling for his phone. He laughed and punched my shoulder, dropping the phone back into his pocket. "Just kidding. Wait, you didn't? I thought you said you wanted to get fucked? Oh, did you top?"

I couldn't help looking at Jeremy, who was looking back expectantly. His eyebrows had been painted white, so I could see just how high they were raised. He had a lei around his neck and hibiscus petals scattered between his ears, one of which drifted down to the floor as he tilted his head at me. "Don't worry, sweetie," he said in a singsong voice. "Someone's got to be on bottom, someone's gotta be on top. Did you have a good time? That's the point."

"Let's start over," I said, sticking out a paw. "Hi. I'm Lonnie. Usually I don't discuss my sexual pro…procliva…" I took a breath and forced my tongue to work. "Pro-cliv-it-ies with people I haven't met."

He laughed and shook my paw. "He can still use big words at one-thirty in the morning at a party. Oh, I like this boy. Where did you find him, Derek?"

"He went to Ford. Sorry—William J. Ford High, same as me. Only *he* went off to some northeastern college." He gave me a thumbs up. "Just got back to the city couple months ago."

"I graduated in December," I clarified, because people usually asked that, but that wasn't what was on the black rat's mind.

"High school." Jeremy turned back to me and smiled even wider, showing his front teeth. "Oh, is *he* the one…?"

"No," Derek and I said at the same time.

"Pity." The black rat looked me up and down, and his pink tail—which was decorated with a red ribbon—waved back and forth. "*I'd* get kicked off the football team for doing him."

I said, "Well, I'm kinda worn out for tonight," because it seemed politer than, "super-flamey rats aren't really my thing."

"Darling," Jeremy said. "That wasn't an *invitation*. It was just appreciation."

"Don't be flattered," Derek said. "He's 'appreciated' most of the guys here."

"But not all." Jeremy held up a finger, the claw painted red to match the trim on his vest. "An important distinction. So Lonnie, tell, tell. Who was the lucky fellow whose open…arms welcomed you to our fair neighborhood?"

He looked across at me, and Derek looked down. "Um," I said. "He was a fox, about six feet tall."

Derek's broad smile wavered, and his eyebrows lowered along with his ears. "A fox."

He didn't say anything else, so I said, "He had on a…a blue shirt."

They both waited. Derek nudged me. "Yeah? And?"

"And what?" I asked.

"Did this vulpine vision have a name?" Jeremy smiled. "Or do you have a different set of social rules for indulging in sexual proclivities than you do for discussing them?"

My ears flicked back. Derek patted me on the shoulder. "Lonnie thinks too much. I bet he's already feeling all tail-down about having sex at a party."

"I just don't want to talk about it." I uncurled my tail and tried to sound indignant.

"My dear," Jeremy said, his smile broadening, "everyone is doing it. Look." He gestured, and I turned to see a ferret stepping off the staircase. "Gilliam! Gilliam, dear!"

The ferret ambled over to join us. "Gilliam, this is Derek, who works in the gym, and his friend Lonnie, who's new in town." We shook paws all around. "Lonnie is rather embarrassed as this is his first McMinaver's party. Would you be a dear and tell him what you were just doing?"

I held up a paw, my ears burning again. "I know. I saw—you don't have to—"

The ferret's paw dropped to his pants, and he grinned. "I got a blow job from Martique. For old times' sake."

Jeremy feigned—I think he was feigning—shock. "Oh dear! Victor was otherwise occupied?"

"Martique said he was getting some from that skunk who's down from Corraponset."

"Mortimer? He's married, isn't he?"

"Married, not dead."

"Touché." Jeremy turned to me. "You see, there's absolutely no reason to be ashamed. You needn't tell us the name if you don't like, but there's no judging at a McMinaver's party. Most of the rest of the time we are really quite terribly boring. I assure you that not telling us your fox's name will only redouble our determination to discover who it was."

"Not for me," Derek said. "If he had a cock and put it in you, that's all I need to know."

I took a breath. "Is it bad if I don't remember? I am still…" I held my finger and thumb an inch apart. "A little bit drunk."

Derek and Jeremy both burst into laughter. "Awesome," Derek said.

"Anonymous sex is the best kind." Jeremy grinned. "That way you can meet a person for the first time twice."

My ears were back and I was looking down at the floor, and that must be why Derek patted me on the back. "Hey, bro," he said. "Next time maybe try a different species at least."

"What's wrong with foxes?" Gilliam put his paws on his hips. "They're lovely."

"His douchy ex who dumped him was a fox," Derek said before I could stop him.

"So much the better." Jeremy smiled at me. "Get him out of your system. How long were you together?"

"Three years," I said. "All through college."

"Then the asshole just up and—"

Jeremy held up a red-tipped paw, and Derek shut his broad muzzle. "Not really the point, though," the rat said as his pink tail flicked back like a whip. "Lonnie here had himself a marvelous time, and we should all drink to that. What do you drink, Lonnie? Bar is closed, sadly, as it's after one-thirty, but there's beer, and the wine isn't as terrible as you might assume if you've been to other parties."

"Just water," I said. If there's one thing I definitely learned from three and a half years of college, it wasn't math or physics or even my ostensible major of geology, nor yet how to keep a boyfriend, apparently. When to stop drinking, though—that I had down to a science.

"Smart boy," Jeremy said on his way to the bar. He took Gilliam by the arm. "He'll be enjoying the breakfast at The Morning After, not just nursing a Bloody Mary."

"The Morning After?" I asked Derek, when Jeremy and Gilliam had gone.

"It's a café where all of Cottage Hill hangs out the day after one of these parties." Derek holds his liquor pretty well, and though I'd been to a dozen bars and parties with him, I'd never seen him falling-down drunk. It helps to be 250 pounds and mostly muscle. Honestly, if he'd been more devoted to football, he probably could've played in the UFL.

"Are you going to take me there?"

"Of course!" He laughed and took another swig of his beer. "That's part of initiation too. So do you really not remember this fox's name, or were you just shy around Jeremy? Don't worry about him, he's a sweet guy, just likes to go all out for the party. I don't know that guy Gilliam, but he seems cool too. Jeremy never introduced me to someone skeezy."

"No, I really don't." I imagined Steven asking me that, not that he would. *You cheated on me*—no. *You slept with another fox and you don't even know his name?* "I thought maybe…" I swallowed. Still a little drunk, just enough that I couldn't keep my unhealthy fantasies to myself.

"What?" Derek nudged me.

"It's stupid."

"It's your first one-night stand. No, it was better. Like a one-hour stand. Come on, bro, I wanna help. What is it?"

I curled my tail against my side, heart beating faster. "I just…I had this idea that it *was* Steven."

Derek stared at me. I thought for a moment he was going to laugh, but he just grabbed my shoulder and pulled me against him. "Aw, Lonnie. It wasn't."

"I *know*." I tried to wrestle away, but fuck, he was strong.

"Did it smell like him?"

"Yeah. I mean, no, but…" I gave up and leaned against his shoulder. "There's…there's stuff you can take to disguise your scent."

At that, Derek did laugh. "You mean like in those James Bond movies? You think Steven works for the CIA?"

"You can get them out of catalogs. On the Internet."

"Look." He let me go and pulled his phone out. "Look, here's his ScentBook page."

I stared at the screen. "Why are you following Steven?"

His thumbs called up my ex-boyfriend's profile. "In case you did something dumb like try to go back to him, I could see what a douchenozzle he is and show you proof."

"Thanks."

"I told you, I'll get you through this breakup." He showed me the phone. "See? He's at the Theatre on the Green. Wait, it looks like he didn't even spell it right."

"They use the British spelling," I said, looking down at the check-in. He was there with Cranston, all right. He hadn't come down for one last fuck. "Dammit."

The bigger wolf put his phone away and clapped me on the shoulder. "It's cool you don't remember who it is, but at least you know it wasn't him. So how'd you get this fox upstairs?" When I didn't answer, Derek said, "I mean, I usually just spot someone hot and say, 'Want to go?'"

"Yeah, I remember." I shake my head. "I think—well, I think I was talking to a raccoon, but I went to get another mojito and when I came back, he was a fox, so I guess it wasn't the same guy, and I..." I stopped, remembering wide eyes and perked ears, though I couldn't place a face around them. "Oh, god."

"What?" Derek looked around the room. "You see him?"

"No." My voice was trying to crawl back down my throat. "I think I said something like, 'I haven't had a good fuck in months.'"

A glass of water met my paw. My fingers curled around it instinctively. "Surely that's not still true," Jeremy's high voice said.

My ears went back again and I lapped at the water. "These big parties," I said, "I can't smell or hear people coming." I turned to see only Jeremy; Gilliam must have gone off to talk to someone actually interesting.

Jeremy patted my shoulder. "It's all right, darling. We've all gone through dry spells."

"Yes," I said, "but most of us don't talk about them to people we've just met." More thoughts crowded through my head. "Oh, no, did I just get a pity fuck?"

"How's that different from a regular one?" Derek asked.

"The pillow talk after," Jeremy said. "You end up lying there thinking, 'does he feel better yet?' and you don't want to say it until the glow's kind of faded, you know, but you know he's not going to say anything until you do because he knows it's a pity fuck too, and so the best thing you can do is just wait 'til he falls asleep and then sneak out." He paused. "Then text him later and tell him how good it was. And be vague about when you can do it again."

"Uh," Derek said, "I know that, but what about *getting* one?"

"Never mind," I said. "Look, it was just a drunken hookup, and I'm sorry it happened."

That wasn't strictly true, but I said it for effect, and it worked. Both Derek and Jeremy looked at me with dismay. "My dear," Jeremy said,

"I know we've only just met, but you're single and healthy, and sex is nothing to be ashamed of."

"Yeah," Derek said. "You needed to get laid."

"I know," I said, with a bit of a growl to my voice.

"What you don't need," the black rat said, "and again, please excuse my forward nature here, is to feel so guilty about this that you don't go out and get laid again. You said it had been a few months. Don't let it be another few. There are plenty of happy, willing boys in Cottage Hill, not to mention Port City itself."

"Yeah." Derek gripped my shoulder. "Come by my bar sometime, I'll introduce you."

Derek's bar, across from his gym, catered mostly to gym patrons for whom I suspected I would be about as attractive as a bowl of rice pudding. "Maybe." I looked around the room, ears flicking back. "Hey, are people starting to leave?"

"Yes, and amazingly, we're all still upright." Jeremy gestured toward me with a flick of his red claws. "If not for Lonnie's adventure and a certain agile skunk in a red feather boa," he licked his lips, "I would say this evening had been something of a disappointment."

Derek laughed. "Like you need a party to get laid."

"True enough!" Jeremy raised his glass. "Anyway, shall we move the party to the Blue Moon?"

I was still looking around the party, though I hadn't yet been able to match black ears with a blue shirt, and it was only when nobody answered the question that I looked back and saw both the big wolf and the skinny rat staring at me. "Oh, me?" I lapped at the water again. "I, uh, if you guys want to go, then go ahead."

"Sure," Derek said, but Jeremy eyed me keenly.

"You're looking for him, aren't you?"

"For who?" My tail bristled up.

"For your fox." Jeremy grinned at me and gestured with his drink. "You want to see who it is."

My ears burned. I stuck my nose in the cup again. "Don't care," I mumbled.

"What did he smell like?" Derek asked.

"Oh, here near the hibiscus and pineapple, he can't remember," Jeremy said. "Come on, let's walk out. The party's dead anyway."

People still milled around on the floor, but the temperature had definitely gone down a touch and I thought the conversation had too. I trusted Derek, and Jeremy by proxy, to judge these things better than I could.

Outside, I confessed to them that my memory of his scent was limited to 'fox,' and that I only really had one concrete example of it.

"Did he leave you his underwear?" Jeremy asked. "Because if you didn't ask for it, then that's just crass."

"No, I, uh." I curled my tail down. "I had to wipe him out of my fur—under my tail—and put my boxers on before I could wash properly. So they sort of smell like…"

"Like his come?" And right there in the street, Derek knelt down and stuck his nose under my tail.

Or tried to, anyway; I jerked away from him and said, "Are you crazy?"

He looked up with a lopsided grin, his tongue hanging out. "Just tryin' to help," he said. "So you barebacked?"

Nobody around us on the suburban street seemed to have noticed. At this time of night, they were all people leaving the party at the huge mansion anyway. I yanked Derek to his feet. "No, but before he put the condom on, there was—look, you can help by telling me which foxes are taller than me."

"Just post something on ScentBook and we'll pass it around," Jeremy said, "That's where everyone goes to catch up on party gossip."

"Isn't that sort of, uh, desperate?" My first reaction was, no fucking way, but the more I thought about it, the more the idea had appeal.

The black rat laughed and rested a paw on my shoulder, and even though we'd just met, I didn't mind the touch. "You'll hardly be the first to look for a party hookup. Don't worry, I'll make sure everyone knows you're not creepy, just wanting to say thank you."

CHAPTER TWO

I skipped the Blue Moon but did go with Derek to The Morning After, a diner that made average eggs, good pancakes, and an excellent Bloody Mary. We sat under the huge pink rooster and they helped me compose my ScentBook post, which for some reason still seemed like a good idea. Then Jeremy talked about his skunk and Derek talked about the date he had that evening with a coyote from the West Coast.

Derek's a good guy, even if I didn't find that out until we'd both graduated. Literally, I was at a post-graduation party, and of course I'd heard about the incident with him losing his spot on the football team, but I hadn't had the courage to talk to him until I had a couple beers in me—or a couple couples.

He always had that shine of confidence about him that I envied and coveted, and hadn't lost it through two years of college and two years of working at the gym. It made him an effective personal trainer, a highly sought-after date, and, most importantly to me, a good friend.

Jeremy I wasn't sure of. His mannerisms felt elaborately fluffy, but I had trouble working out what they were concealing. He enthusiastically contributed to the posting, and immediately shared it from his account as well (he'd already followed me the night before, so I returned the favor and within ten minutes got another ten follow requests), and then engaged in a good half hour of speculation about all the foxes he knew, while I contributed mostly attentive ears and Derek a succinct, "Hot" or "Meh." After each one, Jeremy leaned toward me and I shook my head.

"Might be him," I said. "If he's a fox."

He mentioned jewelry, and while I vaguely remembered ear studs, they could easily have been from any of the other guys I'd talked to that night. In the end, my memory just didn't come back enough to be of any use, so we left it at the posting and he went off to work while Derek and I went to a movie.

Monday came and went with no responses to my post, unless you count the half-dozen guys (only one fox) who offered to help me relive the experience. I replied politely to each one; sitting in the sober, sterile cubicle of the Geological Survey, it was a lot harder to imagine myself just picking up a random guy, especially some of the spelling-challenged mouth-breathers who apparently followed Jeremy's or Derek's ScentBook accounts.

Tuesday I grabbed lunch with Derek: a roast beef sandwich for me, an egg-white omelette for him. I complained about the responses I'd gotten, and he said, "You should go for it. Make a date with one of them. Even the fox if you want."

I scowled, and bit hard into the sandwich. "A, I don't even know them, and B, they all sound like horny sixth-graders. Do I really want to date someone who thinks a personal appeal is an ad for sex?"

"Who said anything about 'date'?" Derek grinned. "Just a fuck, that's all they're after." I looked around the little café, but nobody seemed to care what Derek had said. There was an armadillo a couple tables over, but his ears weren't pointed in our direction.

Derek ignored my paranoia. "Lonnie, you should loosen up. Not every guy you sleep with is gonna be Mr. Right."

"I'd at least like them to be able to *spell* 'right' before I sleep with them."

"See?" Derek grinned a long grin. "That's your problem. Why do they have to spell to have sex?"

"It's not just that. It's..."

He pointed one claw at me. "It is that. They're not going to be your life partner just because they let you in the sack. Lots of different people like sex, and some not very bright people are pret-ty good at it."

"I'm not going to sleep with you either," I said, returning his grin.

"I'm not offering." His grin widened. "I know I ain't too bright."

"You're plenty bright. You're way more street-smart than I am. Or maybe more gay-smart."

"It's got nothing to do with 'smart.' It's just got to do with—"

"I know, I know, loosening up." I finished off the sandwich. "I'm still...not quite there yet."

"You were there last night." Derek leaned forward. "It's been three months. I haven't ever even *dated* anyone for that long."

I lost my grin and flattened my ears. Derek scooted his chair around and patted my shoulder. "Hey, Lonnie, the guy was a jerk."

"He was not a jerk," I mumbled, because Steven wasn't there to defend himself. "It just wasn't going to work out."

He let it go, which is why he's more gay-smart than I am. "All right. I gotta get back to the gym. I have a one o'clock with an adorable arctic fox who doesn't know how good he looks." He winked. "If you want, I can set you up with him."

"After you're done with him, or before?"

He shrugged. "Either way is fine with me."

"You enjoy him," I said.

He pushed his chair back into position. "While you look for a guy you had a drunken fling with at a party."

"Go to your training session," I said. "I'll be fine."

I took my phone out and checked the post again, and of course there was nothing new there, so I headed out into the cool spring breeze. It smelled like rain, so I was hurrying back to the subway when a voice behind me said, "Lonnie?"

I turned to see a black rat in a sober black t-shirt with a store name tag on it. He wore slim blue jeans, so restrained that even though his name tag read "Jeremy," it wasn't until I caught his scent that I recognized him. "Oh, hey."

"Lunch break?" He wasn't doing the flamey sing-song voice either. It was a little weird.

"Yeah." I indicated the gym. "I come by to see Derek every now and then."

Now the musical quality came back to his voice, just a little. "That's sweet you kept in touch since high school."

"Well, you know how Derek is," I say.

The smile pushed up the corners of his eyes, and he became the rat I'd met over the weekend again. "I know how he is with people he's slept with."

"Oh, hey, we never—I mean, I wasn't out, and then I went to college, and—"

"It's okay." He rested a paw on my arm, light fingers through my sleeve. "I know. He told me. Apparently his relationships last longer when sex isn't involved."

"Yeah." I turned and sniffed at him. "So—so you and he haven't—"

Jeremy laughed. "Aren't you sweet! Oh, we slow-danced a few times, and maybe a few times without music, but I'm not the sort to demand an encore, and neither is he. We understand each other well."

I honestly wasn't sure how he'd answered. "Great. Okay, well, I have to get back to work…"

"I'll let you go," he said, and his paw released my arm. "Did you get any answers to your post, by the way?"

"No." I glanced at the subway stop and then did mental calculations in my head. I could spare five minutes, and the rain hadn't started yet. "Just random people offering sex."

"I'd say that's a net gain, wouldn't you?"

Of course he'd say the same thing as Derek. I raised a paw. "I appreciate the help with it. I'll let you know if someone answers."

I'd gone three steps when I felt a light touch on my shoulder. "Lonnie. I'm sure Derek can go through some of the foxes who might've been there."

"Yeah, but he won't." A raindrop brushed my ear. I kept walking. "He's right, I just need to loosen up or something."

He let go of my shoulder, but walked alongside me. "He may be right about that, but that doesn't mean he's right about you finding this fox."

That stopped me. I turned and looked him in his white-accented black face. "What?"

A few more raindrops pattered around us as he talked. "Look, he was your first one-night stand. I know I would just be happy I got laid, but you obviously want to know more about it. So if you're going to have more one-night stands, which is a thing you want, maybe, yes? Then you should find out who he is. Besides, maybe it'll put a nice spring back in your tail, and keep those ears perked up. You're so much cuter that way."

I put my ears up, and then they flushed because he'd called me cute and I put them down again, and then I got them back up because I was processing what he'd said. "So you'll help me?"

"I love a good mystery." He winked and pointed to the subway marker. "Meet me back here for coffee after six?"

"Sure." I nodded, and was amazed at how much lighter I felt as I skipped down the stairs to the trains.

*

I texted Jeremy when I got to the Cottage Hill stop, and he texted me the location of a coffee shop called "Dominic's."

The coffee was pretty good, better than the Geological Survey's break room coffee. Once I'd sat down and lapped at the iced mocha latte Jeremy had recommended, the black rat set both his elbows on the table and leaned across. "So," he said, "I talked to Maxie at work and we came up with a list."

He produced his phone and set it down on the table. I stared over the rim of my coffee cup. "You talked to someone else about it?"

His thin white eyebrows rose. "You posted it rather publicly."

"Oh, right." I buried my nose in the cold chocolatey coffee again and sipped.

"Anyway. Between the two of us, we rattled off twenty red foxes we saw at the party last night. You said he was taller than you, right? About six feet?"

I nodded. "Within an inch or two."

"That took out eleven of them. Of the others, there's Creighton, but he never left Barwyn's side. So sweet. And then there's two I definitely saw most of the time you were upstairs because they were kissing in one of the alcoves and those tails were swishing and curling and…mmm." He paused, no doubt reliving the sight.

"That leaves six?" I prompted.

"Yes. Maxie and I between us know four of them well enough that we could call and say, darling, are you the one who went off with that adorable little new wolf and did you see his post?" He looked up from his phone with a smile. "So we did. And three of them said no, and one said he hooked up and used a condom and he thinks maybe it was a wolf, but he wasn't a hundred percent on it. He, ah, wasn't *just* drunk, I guess. But if he used a condom, he was on top, so we can rule him out."

I coughed. "Actually, um."

The corners of his mouth stretched back. "Oh, that's right, you were on bottom, weren't you?"

He said it in a loud enough conversational tone that I looked from right to left to see if he'd drawn anyone's attention. Fortunately, the only person who seemed to have heard was a nearby ringtail, who'd looked over from his tablet to scrutinize me. He didn't turn away when he caught me looking at him, not until he'd let me see him looking me over, and then he smiled—not at me—and turned back to his tablet.

"Well," Jeremy said. "We'll make Porton our number one, then, shall we?"

"Yes," I said, though I hoped my lover (*one-night stand*, my brain corrected me) hadn't been the fox too drunk-slash-wasted to remember my species. I'd been drunk but at least I'd gotten that right. "And there's two others?"

"Wendell and Cristal." On his phone, I could see the spelling of that name, but Jeremy pronounced it "Kris-TAHL," and accompanied it with a slight but noticeable eyeroll. "Wendell is married to Taylor, a civet, only Taylor wasn't at the party and Wendell was, and he may have gotten a little drunk and played around and now doesn't want to admit it. I know Taylor better than I know Wendell, and, well, they have sort of an openish relationship, but if this was outside that, then Wendell wouldn't tell me because he'd know I'd tell Taylor. And Cristal," again the eyeroll, more noticeable this time, "well, he's kind of a snob. He might not want to admit he fucked someone who isn't a Cottage Hill A-lister."

My ears flicked downward, and Jeremy covered my paw with his. "Oh, sweetie, don't feel bad about that. The only people who care about being A-listers are the A-listers, and believe you me, you don't want to get tangled up in them or you'll spend your whole life worrying about what people will think about every little thing you do and that's no way to enjoy yourself."

That did perk my ears up. "So what else do you know about those two?"

"Well, did your fox have a wedding ring?"

"Maybe." I squeezed my eyes shut and called to mind a memory. Black paws, soft on my shaft. The image made me fidget in my seat and open my eyes. "I don't remember one."

"Wendell might easily have taken his off." Jeremy hummed. "Maxie thinks he's switchy, and I know Taylor is. Cristal, well, that's anyone's guess. So either of them could have topped you." He turned off his phone and sat back. "I suppose there's only one way you can really find out."

I gulped down a little more cold drink. "Go ask them myself?"

"They might easily lie." He smiled at me. "But their scent won't."

"I told you, I don't have anything with his scent on it. Just my boxers, and that's just—oh, no."

The black rat's grin stretched all the way back to his ears. He clasped his paws together. "It's a sexual mystery! I'm so excited for you. I wish I were doing it."

"Tell you what," I said. "You seduce each of them and then I'll run in and..." I looked down at the table. "That'd be pretty weird, huh?"

"You'd be surprised," Jeremy said. "But three times in a row and you'd get a reputation."

"I'm going to get one your way, too." I sloshed the ice around in my drink.

"Yes, but that kind of reputation doesn't make you less popular."

I sighed and tipped the cup to my lips. "That's what I'm afraid of."

CHAPTER THREE

To be honest, there was a time there when I almost gave it all up completely. I mean, none of the three sounded like a prize candidate to me. But I knew myself, and I knew that if I didn't get the guy's identity, it would nag at me for years. There'd never be a better time than right now, this week, and I had Jeremy to help me. I told Derek about it, of course, but he just shrugged and said, "You want me to set you up with a fox, I'll be happy to." I told him he was missing the point and he said he didn't think *he* was.

Jeremy and I started with Porton, the guy who at least thought he might have slept with a wolf at the party. We waited another couple days in case someone replied to my post—nobody did—and because a Friday night would be easier to work a date into anyway.

But to get a date for Friday night, I would have to meet up with Porton on Wednesday night. Jeremy said Thursday was too close. "But I could make the date for Saturday then," I said Wednesday after work, as he was outlining our strategy for that night.

"I'm busy Saturday," Jeremy said, and then before I could ask why he needed to not be busy, he set down his phone on the table and called up a picture. "Here's Porton."

I looked down at a fox with half-lidded eyes and plump cheekruffs, his mouth open as if he were talking to someone. A Starbucks cup had been frozen by the photo halfway to his muzzle. His fur, askew around the cheeks and ears, looked almost as though he'd just woken up. "Nice," I said.

"Stir any memories?" I shook my head, and Jeremy turned the phone off. "Ah well. Was worth a try. Anyway, he knows about your post, so this one should be fairly easy. He's expecting you for dinner just down the street. I hope pizza's okay. I took the liberty."

"Wai—what?" My ears stood straight up and I almost knocked over my coffee. "You made a date for me? I thought I was just going to run into him, talk to him."

"After you'd made the post about a fox and I'd called him asking about the party? That wouldn't look too suspicious, would it? If someone knows you want something, and you don't tell them flat out, they're going to wonder why not. No, I just said you want to have dinner with him to see if any memories come back, and nothing more." He brushed his whiskers back. "I think he was intrigued because I made the date for you. It's possible he might not have been if you'd called yourself."

I looked down the block, but I couldn't see the pizza place. "Why don't I just sleep with him tonight, then?"

The rat's smile vanished. "Sweetie, I told you. McMinaver's parties are one thing. Outside the parties, we're all very normal and, well, moderately restrained. He wouldn't sleep with you tonight unless you really do everything right. So suggest Friday night. Second date, if you play your cards right, should get you the sample you need."

I huffed. "Who says I won't do everything right?"

Jeremy reached over to pat my cheek ruff. "You're adorable. Surprise me."

"Maybe I will," I said, and it wasn't until I was walking down to the pizza place through a persistent light rain that I realized I'd just accepted a challenge to get a stranger to go to bed with me on a first date. Could I do that? I licked my lips, thinking about it. I could at least try. The prospect was enticing, and I liked that Jeremy believed I could—well, I might do it. If I surprised him. I found that I wanted to.

Jeremy would wait for my call or text, and if the café was still open when I was done, we could meet there. As much as I wanted to tell him not to worry, the thought of him being there made me feel more comfortable about this whole deal. For someone I'd only known four days, he instilled a sense of confidence in me that few of my long-term friends did.

Of course, since the breakup with Steven, I hadn't had much contact with any of my—our—friends, and their posts on ScentBook had been fewer and less personal, so I was pretty sure I'd been removed from most of their Friends circles. Derek was the only long-term friend I really had left.

The pizza place was called "Greek Style," and the drawing of scantily-clad athletic wolves around it made me wonder if the name was innuendo. Staring at the drawings while I took my rain jacket off, I didn't at first realize that the ermine host was talking to me, asking if I wanted a table for one, and that a tall, stocky fox was asking me if my name was Lonnie.

"Oh, uh, yeah," I said to him, and then a lame, "Thanks," to the ermine as I followed Porton back to his table.

He introduced himself formally, and I did the same, and we sat across from each other. I searched him for any hint that he might recognize me, but the only thing we had in common was that he was doing the exact same thing to me. Our smells were stronger from the wet fur, but that didn't help me identify him.

The waitress came with a beer for him and took my order for a Diet Coke. I let him order the pizza, with a wave to indicate that anything was fine. "So Jeremy says you just moved down here," he said when the waitress had gone.

"I just got my place five weeks ago." I told him I worked downtown, and he didn't ask what I did.

I waited for him to offer his own employment, and instead he took a drink of his beer and said, "And you had a drunk fuck at McMinaver's?"

"Seriously?" I said. "Does everyone here just talk about sex in public like it's no big deal?"

"It is no big deal," he said, and grinned around his beer, bringing it to the tip of his muzzle and pouring it along his tongue, which he curved into a channel to guide the beer down his throat. Derek used to do that in high school, at least at the one party I met him at, but I hadn't seen him do it since I'd moved down. There was a giraffe at college who said his friends did it too. Steven and our—his—friends were too classy for that.

"It is to me." Thank god the waitress came back with my soda before I could say anything else. I was supposed to get this guy in bed tonight, and the first thing I say about sex is that it's a big deal? Great. Jeremy was right about me. "I mean, it has been. Everyone says I need to loosen up about it."

"Met a lot of people down here?"

I told him about Derek, whom he thought he knew or had at least heard of, and Jeremy, "and Derek's introduced me to a bunch of guys from the gym, and I have some friends at work. We go out for beers once in a while."

He nodded. "Did you move down here for Derek?"

"No! I mean—" I clasped both paws around my soda and resisted the urge to tip it down my tongue. The jocks had a name for it, but I couldn't remember what it was. Channeling? "I knew him from high school, and I'm not out to my family, and I didn't want to go home anyway."

"Where's home?"

"Across the river." I pointed. "Go through Carjack-town past Gutted Factory-ville, take a left and head down the turnpike until all the houses look the same and the street signs are in a precious Olde Style font. Look for the massive hive of department stores and you're there."

He snorted. "I'm from Dairytown, myself."

"Is that a euphemism or a real name?"

"Take your pick. It's not the middle of nowhere, but you can definitely see the middle of nowhere from it. I got tired of hooking up behind the Barn."

I squinted. "Euphemism or real place?"

He grinned at that. "So you and Derek?"

"Oh. We're just good friends. He was the quarterback at my high school until, uh." I paused, and then thought, hell, everyone talks about sex here, right? "He got caught fucking a cheerleader in the coach's office."

Saying the word "fucking" in a public place felt dangerous enough to make my skin prickle, though not enough to raise my fur anywhere but my tail. It also felt oddly liberating, especially when Porton just nodded. "Male cheerleader?"

"Yeah. And actually, 'got caught' is kind of overstating it, too. He left stains—come stains—on the floor and his scent all over the desk. Plus there were security cameras."

Porton whistled. "Surprised they didn't expel him."

"That's Derek. I don't think it bothered him to get kicked off the team. Coach was really the only one who was angry about it, and that's cause they had to bleach the carpet in his office. Everyone else was like, 'hey, it's 2010, boys will be boys and gay boys will be gay boys.'"

"There were still kids getting bullied in 2010. Still are now."

"Yeah, but." I tried to figure out how to say it. "It wasn't that nobody would dare bully Derek. I mean, there was that, too. But nobody would want to. You could call him 'faggot' and he would just grin at you and say, 'yes?'"

Porton nodded. He took another drink of beer, lips around the bottle mouth this time, not showing off. "I didn't come out 'til I was out of high school."

"Yeah, me neither." I realized I was talking about myself a lot. "Did you move here right from high school?"

"Uh-huh. I mean, I'm good with my paws. You don't need a college degree to be a plumber, right?"

"Not last time I checked. That's what you do? Cool. Do you, uh, find it rewarding?"

His fangs showed in a smile. "You ever had to call a plumber?" I shook my head. "Then yeah, I find it very rewarding. I drive a Porsche."

Our pizza arrived just as he asked me what I drive, and I told him I had a little import sedan that was actually at my parents' place because everyone told me not to try to keep a car in the city, and that was when we started eating, so I spent the next several minutes wondering if the car thing was going to be a deal-breaker, and, furthermore, what I had to do to get the date to the point where he'd sleep with me. We were getting along okay, but in a "we'll chat at parties" kind of way, not in a "let's go fuck" way.

Even though it was a "chat at parties" kind of conversation, it wasn't reminding me of the conversation at McMinaver's—or at least of the feel of that conversation, since I could barely remember the words. Maybe I needed to be drunk to be a good conversationalist. Or maybe Porton just wasn't my drunk hookup fox.

He talked about his car while we both chewed through two slices of pizza, and though it was pretty good, with feta and red pepper and olives and sausage, I barely tasted it beyond registering that the cheese was hot enough to burn my mouth.

"Sorry," he said as he polished off the second slice. "I love that fucking car. I can go on about it sometimes, I guess."

"It's okay," I said. "Maybe you could take me for a ride sometime."

His big ears flicked down and then back up. "Sure, if you want."

And just like that, I saw a chance to jump from the conversation to the point of the date. "Is there anywhere nearby where you can really open her up?"

Of course there wouldn't be; I knew that before he shook his head. It'd have to be more remote than the city, somewhere with straight roads and no cops, over the river and through the woods, probably upstate. Dammit. We wouldn't be going upstate, not tonight.

I cut off his description of a place that was indeed upstate a ways to say, "Is there anywhere we could take a little ride tonight?"

For the first time, he seemed really off balance. He shoved a piece of pizza into his mouth and said while chewing, "I mean, not really. There's this one place, but it's half an hour away and I gotta work..."

God, I wished I'd ordered a beer. It would be so much easier to be flirty. "That sounds okay," I said. "I mean, I have to work too, but it's— it's a nice night."

Raindrops still pattered against the window, which we could both hear, but he turned his head to look anyway, as if to point out what a stupid thing it was for me to have said. "Maybe another night."

I picked up a slice of pizza and curled it, sliding it into my muzzle in a way that I hoped would indicate to him that I would perform oral sex happily, especially on him, especially if we went out driving tonight. But he was chewing on his own slice, and either he didn't see me or he ignored it or I was not really conveying the concept of oral sex all that well with a slice of pizza. Steven always said I sucked at Charades.

Oh, well. The only thing left to me was to say, "I'll blow you if we go tonight," but then what if he gave me a weird look and thought I was a creep and then I didn't get to have sex at all? I could go back and admit that Jeremy'd been right. It was definitely easier than—

His foot had brushed my leg, the way a tall guy's feet do when he's sitting across from you at a table. I'd moved my leg politely out of the way. Now his foot brushed me again, and in the midst of my distraction, I hadn't moved my leg. The brushing had become more purposeful, his toes sliding along my pant leg. He'd dried off his foot, so his toes weren't wet from the rain, and the touch was kind of nice.

Porton was not looking at me at all. He was working hard on his third slice, and so I did the same, letting his foot fondle my calf. Moderately restrained, my ass. He was coming on to me hard.

"Sure," I said in response to his suggestion of another night, and then, "So you had a good time at the party too, I heard."

His foot stopped where it was. Then he looked up. "Yeah. Couple too many of those pineapple bombs, and the last half's a blur."

The tip of his tail rose into my view and dropped again, rose and dropped. Mine, lying beside my chair as well, swung back and forth. "Same here," I said. "I'm pretty sure I had a good time, though."

"Same here." He grinned.

It looked like we were both done with the pizza. I gulped some Diet Coke and then leaned forward, looking up at him. "So what kind of place does a plumber have?"

                                         *

It worked. Fuck me—well, we'll get to that—but it worked. We made small talk for as long as it took to box up the pizza, and then he walked me back around to his Porsche.

Nice car, as cars go. For my money, something solid that gets you from point A to points B, C, and D with a minimum of fuss and expense is all I need. But I had to admit that the leather seats were sweet, and the engine purred like nothing I'd ever heard when he started it up. "Will you have to slow down in the rain?" I asked.

"Just the traffic," he said with a laugh.

We drove maybe twelve blocks to a garage, and then walked another four to his second-floor brownstone apartment. "Cool," I said, when he opened the door onto a room I can best describe as "classy bachelor pad," about the same size as my apartment. "You know, when I moved here I was shocked at how small the apartments are, but people told me you just don't spend much time there."

"How big's yours?" He dried his feet with a towel by the door and then held it out for me. When I took it, he tapped a switch on the wall, and track lighting lit the sofa, which I assumed folded out into his bed like my futon did.

"About this size." I rubbed the fluffy towel over my feet, sniffing the lightly vanilla-scented air, and as I did so I saw the doors. And—"Wait a second. You have a *hallway?*"

He walked toward it, tail swishing, and beckoned me to follow him. "Bedroom's down this way."

"Holy shit," I said, hurrying after him, ignoring the cheaply framed bodybuilder posters hanging in the hallway. "I never realized how much I like having a bedroom until—until—"

My mouth dropped open. The bedroom wasn't as big as the living room, but it was painted a deep aqua color, all four walls and the ceiling, and in the center was a king-sized waterbed. I'm sure there were dressers and chairs and shit, but I couldn't look away from that bed. Dark blue sheets shimmered in the soft light that came from somewhere under the headboard, and silvery track lighting (what was it with track lighting?) cast a soft glow around.

"Like it?" he said.

From an aesthetic standpoint, it was not as terrible as it could have been, assuming he wanted the effect of an undersea grotto. But judging it as someone who might very soon be rolling around naked on that bed… "I love it. I'd kill for a bed like that."

His paw rested on my shoulder and squeezed lightly. "What would you do just to spend an hour in it?"

I half-turned. In this room, where sex was not remote, nor mysterious, but expected, where I took it for granted that he'd brought me here to get me out of my pants, the words came more easily. " 'What' I would do is open for discussion," I said, and reached around to his side. "But I know 'who.' "

His eyes caught the silver light. "You kiss?"

"Uh…"

"It's okay," he said, and drew claws down my arm. "You don't have to."

It was more that I'd never thought about it. I hadn't kissed anyone since Steven that I remembered, and of course, really nobody before (not counting that awkward fumbling kiss with that leopard, which I didn't, or the shy pecks with girls in high school, which I also didn't). I was glad enough that he'd taken the option off the table, and even more glad that he was taking the initiative.

This time, I was sure I'd remember all of it: the slow approach while standing, the paws sliding under clothes and through fur, the first brush of his fingers across my pants, the fumbling at the fastenings. He took the lead, and once he crossed a boundary, I followed. I think he picked up on that, because I'd no sooner opened his pants and touched his sheath through his boxers than he shoved his own pants down and put my paw right on his cock.

Right then, I was pretty sure. He was a thick fox, and I didn't think the feel was right. But hell, I wasn't going to just drop his cock and say, "Sorry, not a match." Anyway, hadn't Jeremy and Derek both said I needed to get laid again? Maybe it'd be nicer if I wasn't thinking about whether he was my mystery fox, and just enjoyed the chance to have sex with a new guy.

He let me stroke him to full hardness before he reached to take my pants down, and then we struggled with shirts and he pulled me over to the bed, and things went very fast from there.

His stocky form was mostly muscle, and he was just as attractive naked. That russet and ivory with the handsome black socks always turns me on, even if the blue room wasn't doing it any favors. He seemed to like my plain grey and ivory too, and after a lot of petting, I ended up on my back, head against the headboard, and he knelt in front of me. "I got cuffs," he said. "You into that?"

"Cuffs?"

He gripped one of my wrists. "Paws. Feet too, if you want."

"Oh." I was still too sober to be tied up. "Maybe next time."

"Sure, no sweat." He let go of my wrist and straddled my chest. I opened my muzzle, riding the bed's waves, and he slid his cock into it.

I lapped and lapped and held his balls and felt his knot grow, and his tail swished over my legs and his paws gripped my ears, and I could taste him then. Definitely not the same taste. He had a more oily musk, thick like cheese over the sharp smell of fox. He didn't taste anything like Steven.

"Hey," I said, holding his hips back and pulling my muzzle off him. "You got a condom?"

He stared down at me. "For oral?"

I'd made Steven use a condom the first few months we were dating, and the first three months we were exclusive, too. I nodded. "If you don't, I'll still jerk you off."

My paw around his cock didn't seem to help. He panted, thinking about it, and then leaned to one side and yanked open the nightstand. One rip'n'roll later, his latex-covered member was back against my tongue, and though there was slightly less enthusiasm in his thrusts, he came all the same.

That thawed him slightly. He grinned down and sat back on his haunches, peeling the condom off. "Never heard of anyone using a condom for a blow job," he muttered, but with a smile, his tail wagging lazily.

"Sorry," I said. "I'm just kind of cautious."

He dropped the condom on the nightstand and scooted back, straddling my thighs. "Condom for a blow job, but you're naked on a first date."

I liked being naked, the dangerous edge of intimacy with someone new, and even if he wasn't my party fox, being naked here brought back some of those feelings. "Jeremy vouched for you," I said, and searched for a reason that didn't involve being hung up on an ex-boyfriend. "He didn't give me your disease screening."

He sat back, and I cursed myself right away. I mean, there are less sexy words than "disease," but none I could think of right then. "Ex-boyfriend" would at least have told him I'd once had a relationship. "Also, you're pretty hot," I said lamely.

Porton rubbed a finger along my shaft. "Thanks," he said.

"I'm gonna shut up now."

"Yeah," he said, and curled a paw around me. "I was gonna suggest that."

It wasn't the best paw job I'd ever gotten, but hell, nobody's was really better than my own. Not even Steven, not except a couple times. I lay back and tried not to think about Steven. Instead, I rolled the taste of Porton and latex around my tongue and thought about lying on that couch at McMinaver's with my mystery fox's weight on top of me and his cock driving into me. Harder and harder it drove, and my body squirmed, and my tail curled, and—

"Aaaah!" I bucked up and down on the rolling bed, waves coming up to punch me in the back and legs as I jerked downward against the water. Spatters landed on my stomach fur, white streaks ran down Porton's black paw. I twisted and convulsed, trying to express the current that raced up to my head and down to my toes and back to my groin. And then that, too, was over, and I lay back, panting.

Porton's weight lifted from me. A moment later, he tossed me a small hand towel. "You're cute," he said. "What'd you think of the waterbed? Pretty cool, huh?"

My "disease" comment had hopefully been forgiven. "It was fine. You're good." I wiped most of my come out of my fur and cleaned off my retreating cock.

He traced a claw under my tail while I was wiping myself. "Wouldn't mind doing a little more exploring next time."

"Uh-huh." I shivered a little and thumped my tail on the bed. I should probably have been thinking about having him on top of me, but really what was going through my mind was, *that'll show Jeremy.*

"But I don't think you're the guy I hooked up with at the party," he said.

"No." I rubbed the spatters out of my fur as best I could. "I don't think so either."

From the way he said it, I think he knew when I did, if not before, but he'd gone through with it anyway. I mean, most guys will go ahead if they think they can get a blow job, but I still felt kind of good that he'd been willing to hook up with me. And I'd controlled my thinking about Steven, mostly.

I cleaned up and he gave me directions to the nearest subway stop, with some excuse about not wanting to take his car out again, when I think he really just didn't want me sitting in it smelling of sex. I didn't really want to ride the subway smelling of sex either, not even for just two stops, because I'd been around people who did that and I always swore I never would. So I thought I'd walk. I didn't mind the rain, and it couldn't be that far.

CHAPTER FOUR

"What happened to you?" Jeremy was still sitting outside the café, even though it felt much later than eleven o'clock. "You didn't text me. I was just about to go home."

I couldn't stop panting, even sitting down. I gulped air and then panted again, and tried to make sense of the past half hour. "Um," I said. "I got laid. And then I got mugged. And then I almost got hit by a car."

His eyes widened. "Are you okay?"

"Yeah. I'm fine. He used a condom." I listened to myself give a short, hysterical giggle.

Jeremy didn't laugh. I tried to reach out for his half-full glass of water, and my shaking paw skittered along the table and knocked it over.

Water spilled over the tablecloth. The black rat stood and tossed a bill down on the table. "Come on," he said, grasping my paw in his. "Let's go."

Too rattled to argue, I followed him a block and a half and then up four flights of stairs, to his apartment door. Every step I took I looked around at shadows, wondering if that irregular pattern was a tiger's fur, if that big deer was holding a gun in his coat. It helped that Jeremy kept a paw on my arm and didn't show any fear himself, but by the time I got up to his apartment, I was shaking and I don't think I could've pulled my tail from between my legs with both paws.

Jeremy's place was not quite as small as mine—about the size of Porton's living room, though it smelled nicer, a lavender and honeysuckle aroma that didn't hide Jeremy's own scent. He guided me to a futon folded up into couch mode with dark polished wood arms and a brightly patterned cover, throw pillows in each corner. Across the room stood a range and refrigerator in a small stone-tiled kitchen area, and in front of me, on a glass coffee table, my reflection looked back at me, eyes wide, ears flat.

Seeing it calmed me a little. For one thing, it was kind of scary to see myself looking that way; I understood why Jeremy was agitated, and felt guilty about it. For another, it reminded me that I hadn't been hurt, after all. I'd lost forty bucks or so and my cell phone, and that was it.

"I'm still wet," I stammered, though at least my tail remaining between my legs meant it had stayed dry.

He pushed me down on the futon and went to his kitchen. While I tried to breathe, staring down at the small jade figure of a curled rat on the table, he poured something into a glass, sat beside me, and held it out. I gripped it in both paws and drank without even pausing to sniff it.

The sear of alcohol blasted my nose and throat at the same time. I gulped and then struggled for breath as my eyes watered. "Hhhkkk," I choked, and set the glass down with a hard clink on the table.

"Don't worry about gulping it, dear." Jeremy patted my back. "It's just grocery store bourbon. I use it for cooking or emergencies."

I wiped my eyes and sucked air through my throat. The fire in my head subsided slowly. "Warn a guy, would you?" I coughed.

"Sorry," he said. "I thought that's why you wolves had noses." But even his light mocking didn't change his concerned paw between my shoulders. "Feeling a bit more steady?"

I nodded, and in fact, I did. The fire had spread to a general warmth and relaxation, and my tail unclenched. My paws did too. I hunched forward.

"You don't have to say anything," Jeremy said. "But I find it's helpful to talk about it. The first time it happened to me, I did, anyway."

"First time?" I turned and looked into sympathetic eyes.

"Oh, sweetie, I've been mugged three times. Look, you didn't fight him, you lost—what, some money?"

"And my cell phone."

"No credit cards?"

I shook my head. "All he wanted was cash and the phone."

"Well, the phone is unfortunate. But you had everything stored online, right? You can get a new cell phone easily. Important thing is you didn't fight him, you didn't get hurt."

"Right." I exhaled and then picked up the glass because I thought I needed a bit more steadying.

"That Porton," Jeremy muttered as I sipped the bourbon. "He should've called you a cab."

"It was only twelve blocks," I said.

"Right, and you've just moved here from the northeast." His paw rubbed down my spine, which felt almost as nice as the alcohol. "You walked through the Heights, which he should've told you not to do. If you'd gone down to Merchant and then up, you'd have been fine, it's well lit. Let's be honest, most nights even walking through the Heights is fine, but there's cat gangs there, tigers and leopards."

"Is there a place where there are wolf gangs?" I asked.

He studied my muzzle. "Yes," he said, "but you don't want to go there either, because if you're not one of them you'll still be in trouble. You're feeling better?"

I nodded again, a small nod in proportion to how much better I actually felt. His paw moved up to the back of my neck. "Good," he said. "If you want, you can sleep here on the futon. I'll stay on the floor."

"Oh, no," I said, and started to get up. "I couldn't—"

With surprising force, his paw held me down. "You can. Otherwise I will walk you to the subway, take the subway with you, and walk you to your front door. If you'd prefer to sleep in your own bed, that's fine." He paused. "I could also call Derek to take you home if you want. It's not too late."

"No," I said quickly. "I don't want to bother him. I just—I don't know—" The person I really wanted to talk to was Steven, and if I'd had my phone back I think I would've called him. I didn't know if I wanted to yell at him—"look what happened to me because you dumped me!"—or just cry on his virtual shoulder and hear his voice.

"Stay here," Jeremy said. "When do you need to get up to have time to get back to your apartment?"

Having a problem to solve brought me away from worrying about Steven. I did some quick calculations while he brought his laptop over and opened a guest account for me. "Report your phone stolen," he said, "and I'll set an alarm and get ready for bed."

While I went through the online report form to suspend my phone number and, for the hell of it, ordered a new phone, Jeremy bustled around the apartment. He opened the futon, then brought out a thick quilt and spread it out on the floor.

By the time he'd gotten his temporary bed all set up, my eyes were drifting down. "I'll go home," I protested again, but he clucked at me and said I could barely keep my eyes open, let alone walk, and as he was right about the first, I figured he was probably right about the second, so I just kind of let my eyes slide all the way shut.

"Just sit on the floor here, Lonnie, I'll make up the futon." He tugged gently, and when that didn't work, he put an arm around my shoulders and eased me to the carpet. "Bathroom's over there if you want to wash up."

I did feel muzzy, but my tongue had been seared clean by the alcohol, and anyway I didn't have a toothbrush or anything. So I just sat and picked at the carpet with my claws and then crawled over to the

quilt. "I'll just stay here," I announced, and lay half across it with my eyes closed.

"You will not." The futon creaked as it unfolded into a bed, and then I heard the whip of sheets being unfolded, billowing out over the bed. Breezes ruffled my fur and whiskers. "You're going to sleep in a proper bed. Believe me, I have slept on the floor here many times, dear, it's no burden."

I propped myself up on one elbow and opened my eyes. Jeremy was tucking in the sheets on the side facing me, partly bent over. His pink tail waved over a nicely toned rear. Well, hell, I'd just sucked off a fox I'd met two hours before, and the idea of lying curled up with someone was attractive, even if it wouldn't be who I wanted now. I cleared my throat. "You don't have to sleep on the floor," I said in my best seductive movie voice.

His tail went still. He finished tucking in the sheet, then turned. I let my paw drape over my hip. Then it felt weird, so I moved it to lie on the floor in front of me. But that felt awkward too, so I pushed my elbow back over my side, letting my paw dangle across my stomach.

The black rat took two steps and knelt in front of me, big front teeth showing in his smile. He reached down and touched one of my ears tenderly. I closed my eyes again, already feeling his warm body against mine.

"Oh," Jeremy said softly, and then I felt a kiss and warm breath between my ears. "You are the most precious thing ever."

The warmth and touch retreated, and my whiskers tingled, telling me he'd gotten up and moved back. I opened my eyes and saw him moving to the far side of the futon to tuck the sheets in there. When he saw me looking, his smile brightened. "I'm not going to sleep with you, Lonnie. For one thing, you've had a shock and you wouldn't be in the best frame of mind. For another, I don't take advantage of people like that. For a third, you've just had sex tonight and I'd prefer not to invite comparisons to Porton."

"I wouldn't," I said, but he kept going.

"For a fourth, you're in a grey area for me. You're too much a friend to be a one-night-stand, but not enough to be a friend-with-benefits, and I'm not looking for anything more than that. And for a fifth, you're Derek's friend and he would kill me if I did anything foolish with you. I'm already worried about what he's going to think of tonight."

The flood of information washed over me, leaving relatively little trace. "I'm in a fine state of mine," I said. "Er, state of mind. And what does Derek have to do with it? What did he tell you about me?"

"Nothing I wouldn't have figured out for myself. But I'm always cautious with other people's friends. It's just polite."

"Derek's not my brother, or my boyfriend," I said. "He won't care if you sleep with me. Hell, he'd be thrilled." I put on Derek's voice as best I could. "*Way to go, bro! Another notch.*"

Jeremy straightened, paws on his hips, and his smile was gone. "First of all, 'notch'? Really? Did you move here from 1990 or something? Second of all, I am nobody's 'notch.' And third of all, if you call any of your sexual encounters a 'notch,' or think your friend Derek does, you had better stop expecting to hang out with me."

Shame flattened my ears and lowered my muzzle. "Sorry," I mumbled.

"You're a wee bit intoxicated," the rat said. "I'll forgive you. But I still won't sleep with you. Come on, the bed's ready." He patted it. "Get on up."

I was too tired, confused, and ashamed to argue. I tottered to my feet and clambered onto the futon.

Jeremy knelt on it beside me. "It's going to be all right," he said, and when he rubbed my shoulder, I reached out for a hug. He did put his arms around me and squeeze back, and that, or maybe the bourbon, or both, drew the last bits of tension out of me. I allowed him to pull the sheets up and then spread a blanket over me. "Alarm's set," he said. "I'm just going to do a couple things, but you go to sleep."

I drifted off, but as I did, I thought I heard him talking. "How dare you," he said, and "oh, bitch, you are entirely to blame," and then, "I think you've earned that name." I didn't know who he was talking to, but he sounded pretty pissed. I liked to imagine that it was the mugger, and that that big-ass tiger was apologizing to Jeremy, maybe promising to give me my money back. Or maybe it was Steven, and Jeremy was giving him what for. Imagining Steven cringing in front of Jeremy was a nice dream to fall asleep to.

CHAPTER FIVE

In the morning, I had a very slight hangover that manifested mostly as a headache and an echoing in my ears when Jeremy's shrill alarm went off. That might have been because it was set for heavy-sleeping rat ears and not tossing-and-turning sensitive wolf ears. But I still curled up in the bed for a moment, paws crushing my ears to keep the sound out, while I tried to get my bearings.

The sheets smelled like lavender. The sun was brighter than it usually is when I wake up. I rolled over. There was a glass coffee table, not an inlaid wood one. There were small colorful hangings on the walls and a pride flag on the back of the door. There was a door in the wrong place to be where my closet was with a sign on it saying "FABULOUS PARKING ONLY." In glitter. With rainbow letters.

And on the floor there was a black rat, stretching and yawning. He got up—dressed only in boxers—and smiled. "Need to use the bathroom, dear?" When I shook my head, he disappeared into it.

Right. I'd stayed in his bed, slept in—I checked—yes, slept in my clothes. He hadn't undressed me. Why was I thinking I'd been naked in his bed?

Oh, right. Porton, whose bed smelled like Porton—oily fox musk—who thought I was stupid for asking him to cover his cock before he came in my muzzle. And then the walk home, the corner, the iron paw on my shoulder and the hiss in my ear.

I lay back in the bed and closed my eyes. That wasn't going to happen again. Certainly not in Jeremy's apartment. Jeremy had taken care of me, had let me sleep in his bed, had yelled at Porton.

At least, I remembered him yelling at someone. I didn't worry about it, though, just thanked him when he came out of the bathroom, thanked him again as he offered coffee and breakfast, saying I'd grab Starbucks somewhere on the way home, thanked him again as he opened the door, and then impulsively hugged him before I left.

"Well, thank you, dear," he said, and smiled.

"I really appreciate it. It is nice to feel…looked after." My tail even had some wag in it.

"You'll do fine." He touched my muzzle lightly. "Just be careful, don't let the assholes get you down, and don't *be* an asshole. You'll be fine. Coffee Friday after work?"

"Um…"

"I would let you figure it out, but I don't know when you'll have a phone again."

"Oh, right." God dammit. "I ordered one last night. Yes. Coffee Friday. I'll…I'll set a reminder or something."

"Good. See you then."

I thought all the way back on the subway that I didn't know what I'd have done without Jeremy. I mean, ignoring that without him I wouldn't have been walking through the Heights or whatever anyway. He'd really gone out of his way to help me out, and he hadn't really even asked any questions.

It wasn't until I'd showered and changed and gotten to work that something about the evening started to bother me, though I couldn't quite put it into words. To be honest, it wasn't until after lunch, because once I got my coffee at work and got back to my cube, Derek called me.

"Hey, why aren't you answering your phone?" he asked.

"Didn't Jeremy tell you?"

He paused. "Jeremy has your phone?"

"No. Some tiger in the Heights has it."

There was a longer pause. "You…went on a date with a tiger from the Heights?"

"No."

"Did Jeremy set that up?"

"No, listen." I stood up and looked around my cubicle. My co-workers were all immersed in work at their computers, most with headphones in. I crouched down in my three ineffective walls, feeling like a cub in a play fort, and whispered, "I got mugged."

"Again? Way to go! No pics this time?"

"What?" The cord of the desk phone pulled at my cheek ruff. "No, not f—not that! Mugged."

"Oh. Oh, *shit*. You okay?"

"Yeah, I'm fine. I lost my phone and about forty bucks. Jeremy took care of me."

"Uh…took care of you?"

"We didn't sleep together. He wouldn't let me." My whiskers caught motion and my nose caught the scent of the guy padding toward me. I straightened up. "I'll call you back."

My boss, Kevin, leaned over the edge of my cubicle. "On your own time, please."

"I got mugged and lost my phone," I said, desperately trying for sympathy to get out of being in minor trouble.

Kevin is a big mountain lion who's always wearing a colorful tie, like to prove that he's not just a government stooge, he's a government stooge with colorful ties. We all have to wear ties and I only have two, so I rotate mine. I've been at the Geological Survey for just over a month and I think Kevin's worn one tie twice that I've seen.

Apart from the tie thing, he's an okay guy. I mean, this is my right-out-of-college first office job, and so I don't have a lot to compare him to, but he meets with us—his team—once a week, gives me plenty to do, and answers questions when I have them. Oh, and he does like to walk around and see what his team's doing.

I'd never been caught making a personal call before. When I had my cell phone, I'd just walk outside for a break. I'd also never broached any personal topics with Kevin before, so I was hoping this wouldn't get more awkward than it already was.

When I told him about being mugged, his reaction wasn't really what I was hoping for. "Where were you?" he said.

"The Heights."

"Oh yeah, you can't walk around there at night. I mean, you can't. I probably can't either, but you definitely can't."

Martine, a lithe marten who's sharp as a whip, poked her musteline head over the cubicle wall. "I got mugged down by Broadside Park."

Kevin jerked a thumb toward his chest. "Central Park once, and West Side once." He grinned down at me. "Congrats. It's like a Port City rite of passage. What'd you lose? Just the phone?"

"Some cash," I said. "Forty bucks."

"Not bad," Martine said, and for the next fifteen minutes we discussed the safety guidelines and etiquette of being mugged. I was pretty pleased to learn that I had followed the rules ("give the guy what he wants and don't get mouthy," to which I did not say that earlier with Porton I'd done both, but that thought was probably a good sign that I wasn't going to be traumatized by the mugging).

Over lunch, I went to the store to see if I could pick up my phone, but they said that the one I'd ordered wasn't one they had in stock, and because I'd already placed the order, they couldn't change it. So I was without a phone until Monday. I started to get annoyed at that, and actually almost yelled at the clerk before I caught myself. It didn't help that she was a scruffy fennec with an attitude, the kind I was still getting used to in Port City. "Can't help you," she said, and then was on to the next customer.

Derek came over Thursday night and brought takeout. He grilled me to make sure I was okay until I swatted at his muzzle and told him I'd be fine. "Yeah, well," he said. "I feel kinda responsible for you. You know, bros before nose." He tapped his nose.

The sentiment was clear enough that I didn't ask him what the hell he thought that meant. Maybe "keep your bros in front of your nose" or something. It was cute, anyway. "I moved here to be independent," I reminded him.

"You didn't call Steven, did you?"

I shook my head slowly. That was a lie. I'd called him twice from work, and both times the call had gone through to voicemail. The first time I didn't leave a message. The second I just said, "Hey, it's Lonnie. I just lost my phone so I don't have it anymore," and then there was a long pause while I worked out whether I wanted to tell him I'd been mugged, which would sort of force a sympathy call from him, or if I just wanted to see if he'd want to talk to me again, and then I felt kind of disgusted at myself because I knew he didn't want to talk to me, so I just said, "Bye," and hung up the phone.

"Good." Derek had brought beer, too, and he lifted one in a toast. "That's the kind of thing an ommie would do. What were you doing in the Heights anyway?"

Of all the things Derek did, using that word probably bugged me more than anything else. But he'd brought food and beer, and so I didn't say anything, just nodded my head and made sure I kept my ears up as I told him about the date with Porton, giving him lots of detail about the fox's thick cock and rough paws, which he liked.

"Why didn't he blow you?" he wanted to know.

I shrugged and just said he didn't offer. "Next time, you get as good as you give," Derek said, and though the way he said it made me laugh, I filed the advice away. I hadn't even thought to ask.

Friday I picked up the phone to call Steven again and then put it down. As much as I hated Derek's words, I did feel like a little omega wolf crawling back to the alpha who'd already kicked him out, and I hated that feeling more than I hated not being able to talk to Steven. For god's sake, it had been a month. He'd called to clear up something about a bill that needed to be paid, I'd told him I'd gotten an apartment in Port City, and he'd said he might drop by, in that aloof way that meant he never would. I said he was welcome to, which I probably shouldn't have, and then I got caught up in life and Derek showed me around, and then he took me to a party and I had sex with a fox I could barely remember who smelled kind of like Steven.

And I'd met Jeremy, who'd taken care of me Wednesday night and had settled me down. Leaving work Friday, as I hurried to the subway, my tail wagged. I didn't quite realize why until I thought about sitting down for coffee with the black rat across from me. Derek was sweet and we were friends, but I kept having the nagging feeling that we were only friends because we'd both been gay at the same high school, and because Derek was just friends with everyone. His gym friends had been nice enough to me, but none of them had asked me to come get coffee with them. My co-workers were fun to go out with, but they were married or dating and had kids and mortgages and vacations and season tickets to the theater. Jeremy was the first guy I'd met who really liked me for my personality and wanted to hang out with me more.

I walked up to the café with my question about Wednesday night in my head, and started to ask it when I noticed the garment bag hanging off the back of the chair he'd gestured me to sit in. "What's this?"

"I guessed at your size," he said, "but I'm a pretty good guesser. Go ahead, try it on."

The bag held a blazer, a soft velvet green one with a satin lining. On the breast pocket, embroidered in gold, a small letter "C" stood out. I slipped my arms into the jacket and pulled it around my midsection, then let it hang. It sat perfectly on my shoulders, the cuffs coming just to the base of my thumbs when I let my arms down, and I liked the smell of it, the rich velvet. I felt glamorous, and snuck covert glances around the café to see if anyone else was looking at me (they weren't). "How's that?"

Jeremy just gazed at me and sighed. He wasn't wearing the red vest from his store, but had on a soft yellow shirt with a loose collar that hung open around his black chest ruff, and a filmy reddish-orange scarf draped around his neck. "Gorgeous," he said. "But you need a better tie. And shirt."

My tie was plain blue, and the shirt was light green. Without the jacket, they looked fine; beneath the forest green, Jeremy was right, they looked bad. I turned one more time in the jacket, then took it off and replaced it on the hanger. "What is this for?"

"Do you want coffee or should we go right to the store?" he said, looking up.

"What store?" I sat down, not committing either way.

He finished his coffee and waited, grinning. "All right," he said. "Looks like finding out is more important than coffee."

We carried the garment bag to his car and then walked two blocks down to a store named after some guy I'd never heard of. I squinted at the words on the door as we walked through, started to ask who it was, and then stared around me.

The store smelled like money, but not in a posh designer kind of way where you could smell the crisp new bills and see it in the clean lines and starched collars of the shirts. It smelled like antique money, like paisleys and colorful stripes and shirts I might have seen in old daguerrotypes, updated to the modern day. It smelled bright and colorful, a mix of fresh linen and silk and a light flowery perfume underneath it, but what made it smell like money was the cleanliness of the air. In the ceiling were state-of-the-art filtration units, and they didn't just give those away.

I could see where Jeremy did a lot of his shopping. Rows of shirts arranged by color vied for my attention, and in the center of the floor, a stand of ties streamed out like a rainbow fountain.

"Here," Jeremy said, appearing at my side with two shirts, the first a solid black with a sheen in it that rippled as it moved, the second a light bluish-grey with a subtle white pattern worked through it. "Let me see how these look."

I stood obligingly while he held them up. "Mmm, the black is nice, isn't it?"

"I don't look good in black." The words came somewhat automatically.

"Nonsense, who told you that? You'll look fabulous with this shirt, that jacket…" He held up the black shirt again, examined it thoroughly.

"I thought black was just for emo hispters."

His scrutiny slid upward to my muzzle. "Not a Charles Perrault black. Really, what do they teach you up in the northeast?" And then he must have seen what I was thinking, because he said, "Oh. Your ex."

"I grew up in the burbs. He taught me about fashion."

"Well, excuse my saying so, dear wolf, but he was wrong about certain things. In fact, I think there is quite a good foundation to call his general judgment into question."

My ears flushed, and lowered, but I couldn't keep from grinning. Jeremy whisked the black shirt away and brought it to the tie fountain. "Not to press on a painful memory," he said as I walked up, "but how did it go down?"

I looked over the various patterns of ties, the plain stripes, the solid colors, the intricate patterns and subtle patterns and fifty shades of purple. Jeremy was picking up greens, and had taken out his phone to compare to a picture of the jacket. "He dumped me for a lion who'd gotten into Whitford Law."

"That does not improve my opinion of his judgment one bit."

"I thought you were going to say, 'one whit,' " I said.

He gave me a look as black as his fur. "I'm only letting you say that about me because you're telling a painful story about a terrible cad and how you disentangled yourself from him."

"To be fair," I argued, "Whitford Law, you know, and I'm just a geology major because I had a rock collection as a cub and I like to know how things get made. I mean, I don't have a *plan* or anything like that. I lucked into the job down here."

"Plans are overrated." Jeremy picked up a black tie with green spots on it and held it up to the shirt. "What do you think? Oh, it's fine to have a plan for the evening, but a plan for your life? How do you plan for something that's going to be completely different in a year or five?"

The tie looked like something I might have worn in high school. "Is there anything less…spotty?"

"Spots are whimsical, dear. They're fine. But if you don't like, hm…" He browsed through the fountain. "How long were you together?"

I picked up one of the ties and rubbed the fabric between my fingers. "Almost three years." He didn't respond, so I went on. "Freshman year we met at the LGBT mixer. Sophomore year we lived in the same dorm and started dating. Junior and senior years we lived together off-campus."

"So he broke up with you at graduation?"

"Just after." I rubbed a flame-red tie between thumb and forefinger. "We were going to move out of our place anyway because he was getting a job closer to the city. He told me three weeks before we moved that he was getting a different roommate."

"Classy." The rat held a solid green tie up and then put it back. "At least you didn't walk in on him with the lion."

I wasn't seeing the ties anymore. "Kinda wish I had. Then I'd be able to be angrier at him."

Jeremy stopped looking through ties long enough to roll his eyes. "He gave you the 'friendly break-up'?"

"I don't know if I'd describe it quite like…yeah, maybe on second thought…"

"'There's nothing you did wrong'? 'I'm changing as a person'?"

I coughed to hide my surprise. "Were you there?"

"Honey," Jeremy said, "I've been there for sure." He shook his head and beckoned me to follow him to another rack of ties.

"He said we'd become different people, and our journeys had taken us down different paths. And he quoted the Bhagavad Gita."

Jeremy's eyes widened. "That's a new one on me, dear. Is it like quoting the Bible?"

"For pretentious college students."

He laughed and picked up a bowtie. "There's a little bit of anger. That's healthy. Mmm, definite possibilities here. Can you tie a bowtie?"

"No."

"Can you keep one on once it's been tied?" He saw my smile and reached up to touch my nose. "Bowtie, dear. Just the bowtie. I don't need to hear about your other talents, not while we're in the middle of shopping."

"That's wordplay, too," I pointed out.

"It's sexy wordplay, and that's passable."

I grinned. "Ha. Well, yes. I can keep on a bowtie."

"Good. I think this is your winner."

The bowtie was the green of the jacket with light white flowers on it that Jeremy said were fashionable. "What is this for, anyway?" I asked, going back over to the tie fountain.

"Tomorrow night." The rat followed me and sat there while I looked through some ties for work.

"Where are we going tomorrow night?"

"Skylight. It's a club uptown."

The clerk near us, a lean arctic vixen in her blue summer fur, said, "Ooh, lucky you. Ever been?" I shook my head, and she said, "You are in for a treat. How did you get in?"

This was addressed to Jeremy, who said, "Friend of mine tends bar there. He put us on the list."

"Lovely." She asked if we were shopping for both of us, and Jeremy said it was just me, and she recommended another shirt which I ended up getting because I didn't have many nice shirts, and Jeremy was right, I should get more.

At the register, he tried to pay, and I pushed his credit card aside. "I can afford this. You got me the jacket."

"The jacket only cost me a favor, sweetheart." He smiled and put his wallet back. "But I won't insist, if you want to buy them."

"I do." I gave my credit card to the clerk. "How many people owe you favors around here?" I coughed. "Besides me, I mean."

"I don't keep count." Jeremy smiled. "I just keep in touch. People are sweet and if they can help you out, they will. You'll make more friends if you keep coming around Cottage Hill."

"Thanks," I said to the clerk as she handed me a slip, and I scrawled my name on it, trying not to look at the amount. I think it was as much as I spent on all my clothes in the past year. She gave me the bag with my shirts and ties in it, and Jeremy and I walked out. "I don't know about that," I said as he held the door for me. "I've been here a month and you're the only real friend I've made."

"Yes, but that's because you were hanging out with Derek at the gym and you're not a muscle boy." When I started to protest, he cut me off. "Spare me the 'wolf way' talk. You don't have to be a muscle boy because you're a wolf, any more than I have to be a 'hipster,' as your ex would call it, because I'm a black rat. I just enjoy fashionable things and music I can dance to."

"I used to go dancing with Steven," I said before I could help myself, and then flattened my ears.

Jeremy didn't upbraid me, though, just asked, "What kind of dancing?"

"Swing, ballroom."

"Ever go to a techno club?" I shook my head, and he smiled. "I'll take you sometime, if you like."

"Do just-friends go out to techno clubs?"

He turned with an amused smile. "Yes, they do. They don't go into the locking stall in the bathroom together at techno clubs, but they certainly dance together."

That reminded me obliquely of the question I was going to ask him. "About Wednesday night…"

He tensed and stopped at the corner even though the light was green. Cars roared by behind his concerned frown. "Are you okay?"

"I think so. I mean, everyone acts like it's normal. But it's not about the mugging. It's just something that I wondered about. I mean…" I rubbed my muzzle. Now that I was on the verge of saying the words, they sounded strange and silly to me. I forged ahead anyway. "You didn't think I had much chance to have sex with Porton. But you just kind of assumed I was at his place, and didn't even ask me how it happened or anything like that."

He relaxed and chuckled. "I did have some confidence in you, dear."

"I appreciate that…" I scratched my ear. "But…well, no, okay. I guess I'll just…I mean, thanks."

"You're welcome." He flicked his tail and smiled, and led me across the street and back to his car. "Now, what scents do you have?"

My scent powders met with his approval, so he declared our shopping done. We had dinner at a nice Italian place where he explained to me a little more about the plan for the next evening. Skylight, an exclusive club at the top of the Waterford Tower downtown, sometimes had "Gay nights," and when they did, Cristal was almost always there. So Jeremy had called in a favor from a friend who knew a bartender there and had gotten my name on the list for Saturday night so I could get in.

"You're not coming?"

He shook his head. "I have confidence in you," he said. "From what I hear, Cristal likes well-dressed bottoms."

My ears warmed. "So I just walk up to him and say, 'I'm a bottom'?"

"No." He produced a white handkerchief with blue checks and held it out to me between two fingers. "You fold this and wear it in your right back pocket. It tells him you're open to casual sex, and wearing it on the right means you like receiving. Leaves it open to…" He fluttered his fingers. "Whatever."

I took the handkerchief and turned it over. Jeremy was doing a lot for me, and I couldn't quite figure out why. He'd answered my question about Wednesday night, or had pretty much answered it, but I still wanted to know—well, I just wanted to know more about him. "I heard about this code. Let me just—oh." I'd reached for my phone to look it up, but of course I didn't have one.

He smiled sympathetically. "Trust me. Just leave it hanging out of your pocket. And be yourself. You're charming, and there's no reason Cristal wouldn't at least dance with you. Who knows? Maybe you'll strike up a conversation."

"He sounds like kind of a jerk. I don't know that I want to talk to him, let alone…"

"Oh, give him a chance. He's very image-focused, true. But that doesn't mean he's a bad guy. Look at me."

He fingered his yellow linen shirt, looking down. Fishing for a compliment, or just proud of his fashion sense? I shifted the argument to semantics. "There's a difference between being all about image and just wanting to look good."

"Yes, I agree. So give Cristal a chance, will you? If he's your fox, then you must have seen something in him, right?"

He hadn't engaged me in the semantic argument, but had brought the conversation back around to me, and had hit on the exact point that had occurred to me. I felt again those warm arms around me, the labored breath past my ear. "But if he wouldn't admit to it…"

"From a public message? I mean, I'm not even sure he checks ScentBook, dear. It seems very common for him. Not that I'd know."

"I lived in the northeast for four years, remember? I know from snobs, and that sounds like a snob."

"True, true. Well, I think you'll like him, or at least you'll appreciate him." He rested his elbows on the table. "Is this because your Steven was a snob?"

"No. Well—"

I got lost in thought and forgot about finding out more about Jeremy. I even forgot I was supposed to keep talking. Jeremy interrupted my thoughts politely a moment later with a paw on mine. "Didn't mean to touch a nerve there."

"I'm okay." I pulled my paw back, more sharply than I should have. "It was months ago." Barely, but two and a half is still technically a plural.

"I don't presume to know what works for a breakup for everyone," Jeremy said, "but what worked for me was getting out there and having sex with a lot of people who weren't my ex."

"I can't imagine anyone breaking up with you," I said. It came out glibly—thanks, every romantic comedy ever—but I wondered if he'd respond in kind. He'd been flirty with me but had refused an invitation to sleep with me.

"Yes, well." He smiled. "Neither could I. Which is why it was a bit of a shock. But, you know, *que sera sera* and all that, and anyway, I'm happy now and he's happy and it's all worked out for everyone."

I tilted my head curiously. "Do I know him? I mean, did I meet him?"

"Goodness, no. He moved out to Crystal City three years ago to be a model-slash-actor. If you bought an issue of 'Home Beauty,' let me see, in April of last year, and you noticed an ad for Dimension underwear, or if you happen to stop in at the Starbucks on Recopa Street in Upper Silver

Hill, then you would have seen him." He leaned back. "He's worked his way up to store manager. *So* proud."

"Rat?"

His ears twitched, and he brought one paw up to rub along them. "I am *quite* done with my own species. No, he's a lemur. I do miss that long tail sometimes." He sighed, then focused on me. "And when I do, I find a big cat or a ringtail. You see? Easy."

"It's not that easy," I said.

"Well, no, not after only months—not many, I'm guessing—and anyway, Kiko and I only dated for half a year. Time heals all wounds, young wolf."

Maybe that was all there was to it. Maybe he was just an experienced guy passing on wisdom and help to a young wolf. I hoped so. Because if he wanted something other than sex from me, I couldn't tell what it was. Buying me a jacket, setting me up on dates and in an exclusive club…it was a lot of trouble to go to for someone you'd just met.

CHAPTER SIX

Saturday afternoon I tried on my outfit and had to admit it looked pretty good. When I pulled out the handkerchief and ran the blue-checked fabric over my paws, it occurred to me that now, at home with my computer, I could look it up.

While I was at it, I checked my ScentBook account, which I usually used only from my phone. Logging in involved a lot of tedious remembering of passwords, and I almost gave up, but finally I got in. And there was a message from Steven.

He'd sent it Wednesday night, probably right about the time I was sucking off Porton. It just asked if I was doing okay in Port City, and commented that I seemed to be meeting people. I heard Steven's light sarcasm behind it, and got that feeling that I wasn't living up to his standards. So I typed out a long message about how I was fine and making lots of friends here and studiously ignoring the fact that I'd posted basically a "Connections" ad on my ScentBook account ("Me: drunk-off-my-ass five-foot-five wolf new in town. You: drunk-in-my-ass six-foot fox, handsome, smelling like flowers. If you want to connect again, message me." Not what I really posted, but what I felt like I'd posted. Come to think of it, if I had actually posted that, maybe I'd feel better about myself, or at least funnier.). But I hadn't finished that response before I felt like I was protesting too much, so I deleted it and just wrote that I was fine and actually would have replied sooner, but I had a cock in my mouth. Then I laughed at myself and deleted that, and just wrote, "Fine, how are you?" and then I decided I couldn't ask him how he was because he might start telling me about Cranston, and I should really be okay hearing it but I didn't want to right now, so I deleted that too, and then I finally decided I would deal with it later and I closed the window and went to look up the handkerchief code.

There certainly was a "handkerchief code," but it seemed to be used only sporadically, and I couldn't find "blue-checked white" on there anywhere. The right pocket was the "receiving" pocket all right, but there were three different kinds of lightish blue that the handkerchief could have been. Maybe there was a specific code for this club, or this neighborhood.

It came down to whether I trusted Jeremy or not. I called Derek from my land line to sort of roundabout ask him what he knew about the handkerchief code, and he said he'd never used it and didn't know anyone who did. "So you're over that fox?" he asked.

"Well, uh. Actually I'm trying to track down the second suspect."

"Suspect?" He laughed, which got my fur up. "Sounds like you're investigating a crime instead of a good time."

"Forget it," I said.

"Hey, wait, wait, bro, chill. Where you going?"

"This exclusive club called 'Skylight.' Jeremy pulled some strings and got me in."

He huffed. "Never heard of it."

"Well, it's not a muscle bar," I said, even more annoyed at his tone. What, was he jealous of Jeremy's influence?

"I go other places," he said. "Look, you want to meet a nice guy, I'll take you down to O'Shea's. Lots of regular guys hang out there. You don't have to go to some snooty bar uptown."

"Regular guys," I said. "Why didn't you take me to this place before?"

"I took you to McMinaver's, for Chrissake."

"Which is why I'm going to this 'snooty bar uptown'!"

He exhaled. "I'm just sayin', instead of trying to find a guy who fucked you while you were both drunk, you could try to find a guy you like when you're both sober. Or mostly sober. I dunno if you should stay a hundred percent sober."

His attitude was getting on my nerves. I was doing all this cool, bold stuff, and where was the guy who'd been so encouraging a week or two ago? "Why not? Because I'm boring when I'm sober?"

"Jesus Dog, Lonnie, what's with you? You have to jump all over everything I say?"

"Then stop saying stupid things."

When he spoke again, his voice was a low growl, exasperated. "Well, have fun up there. I hope this fox is as smart as you are."

I felt bad right away. "Look, I didn't mean—"

"No, I'm sure you know what you're doing better than I do. I'm just a dumb muscle wolf. Go on, have fun. I'll see you tomorrow, maybe."

I drew a paw down the line of the jacket. Maybe Derek was right. Did I really need to dress up like this? It wasn't me, it was Jeremy dressing me up, and who was he, anyway? Not even a date, just a friend. But he didn't know me like Derek did.

The smart, the sober thing to do was to call Jeremy to tell him I wouldn't need to meet him to do up the bowtie. But he wasn't answering his phone. And as I was turning to hang up, I caught sight of myself in the mirror. I looked good. I looked really good. Even without the bowtie, I thought, the jacket was elegant and the shirt was daring and when I perked my ears up, I had sort of a "master spy on vacation" look about me.

You know what? Fuck Derek. I was going to go to the club and hit on Cristal. Maybe the Lonnie he knew wouldn't have done that, but then, maybe I wasn't the Lonnie he knew anymore.

*

Jeremy tied the bowtie and then made me sit down while he brushed out my tail, sprinkling a sandalwood-scented powder in it. "Should've told you to take care of this," he said, ignoring the looks from passers-by in the small public park below the Skylight's building.

The sun blazed through the afternoon sky and glittered off every eye turned my way. "Do we have to—ow—couldn't we go inside?"

He held my tail at the base and drew the brush through it. "Plenty of people get their tails brushed in public," he hummed. "It's almost done."

"Yeah, but most of them get to sit in their stroller after." I forced myself to sit still, panting. "And the brusher isn't usually wearing a fishnet halter top and cutoff jeans shorts."

"It's a hot day," the rat said. "Put your ears up. It's worse if it doesn't look like you're enjoying it."

"It looks worse if I *am* enjoying it," I said, but I forced my ears upright anyway. "And I know it's hot. This jacket doesn't come with air conditioning."

"The price of fashion," he replied, and finished by brushing the tip out so roughly that I felt the jolts up my spine.

"All right," I said when he paused, and tried to yank my tail away. Jeremy held on for a moment and then let go. I stood and looked down at him, wagging my tail through the warm air. "I don't want to go in there all panting."

He stood to brush down the arms of my jacket. "The lobby's air-conditioned, and anyway, you can get a drink as soon as you go in." His smile rose to meet my eyes. "You look so good that even if he is your mystery fox, I don't think he'll recognize you."

"Thanks. It's mostly your doing."

"Oh, I picked the clothes, but you're pulling it off." He turned me around, dusted off my back, and then checked the handkerchief in my pocket. "Go get him, stud," he said.

Hot as it was, I paused to look up at the building. An old-style hotel called The Waterford, it stood proudly in ochre stone with white curlicue reliefs around the windows and an elaborate marble doorway over which the name presided, carved in elegant gold script. Though clearly old—a sign nearby proclaimed it had been founded in 1888—the stone glowed in the afternoon light and its reflections shone back from the steel-glass skyscrapers that surrounded it as nieces and nephews might surround an old uncle, distinguished in top hat and bowtie.

I placed a paw on my bowtie, which felt as though it might spring apart at the least provocation once I left Jeremy's side. My eyes traveled up the old, stately hotel to the gleaming jewel at the top, where colored lights were just visible over the reddish-orange glow of approaching sunset, where hedges showed over the left and right sides, where a pure white building with an angled roof sat in the center like a small cap, where the word "Skylight" was written in a handwriting font. It seemed very high up, even amid the taller skyscrapers.

Jeremy's paw patted my tail. "Just be casual," he said. "Be yourself. You're as good as any of them."

I smiled. "I don't know if I believe that."

"You don't have to. Well, you do eventually, and you should because it's true. But you just have to act like it."

"Act like it. Right." I squared my shoulders, took a breath of warm, humid air, and walked forward through the elegant gold-trimmed glass doors.

The Waterford lobby greeted me with a rush of cool air, as promised. From all the posh paintings and gold satin drapery, this was clearly a hotel for people with more money than I had, or was likely to make over the totality of my life, for that matter. Soft music played, something classical that my mother would've recognized, and the people sitting around the lobby all had a detached, preoccupied air, whether bent over their tablets or reading the Business Weekly. Conversations were hushed and the whole lobby smelled clean, the way interior spaces do when they're pumped full of Neutra-Scent. Even government buildings don't usually get that treatment. I had only been in a couple places that did: a casino, on my one trip to Park Place, a fancy restaurant Steven had taken me for our second anniversary, and the Charles Perrault store with Jeremy.

I rubbed my nose as the little tingle of too much Neutra-Scent made it itch, and turned past gilt-framed impressionist paintings and the black marble counter. I'd just taken another step forward when a uniformed black-masked ferret stepped up to me silently on the plush wine-dark carpet. "May I help you, sir?"

His servile attitude unnerved me. "Uh. Skylight?"

"Of course, sir. Right this way?"

He set off slowly, glancing over his shoulder to make sure I was following. I wanted to say, *you don't have to take me there, just tell me where it is*, but he was already on his way, so I hurried after him, looking around to see if anyone was staring at the guy who was making a hotel employee show him around.

Past one of the grand marble pillars we went, to a small elevator lobby. The ferret stopped and turned, gesturing with the intensity of a museum guide. "This side is to the rooms. Are you a guest of the Waterford?" I shook my head. "Those are for guests only. On this side there are two elevators that go to the Skylight Lounge directly and make no other stops."

"Thank you," I said.

He smiled, said I was welcome, and walked without hesitation back to the front of the lobby. I stood in front of the elevators, whose doors were carved with reliefs of sea creatures leaping and playing. The air conditioning had slowed my panting, but I thought I would give it another minute.

Shit, should I have tipped that guy? I only had fifty dollars on me and that was my available cash for the night. Anyway, what should I have given him? A five? A ten? He just walked me twenty feet, for crying out loud.

Don't worry about it. I breathed in deep, stood straight, and pushed the button for Skylight.

My first impression on getting out of the elevator was, as usual, the smell. No Neutra-Scent up here: there was alcohol, lots of it, and only four people in the hallway. They seemed to be two straight couples, badger and mouse, in suits and dresses that were certainly nice but not terribly elegant (I thought with my newly-discerning eye, and then mocked myself; how the hell could I know?). Just beyond them, facing them and me, a polar bear in a white tuxedo blocked a door over which "Skylight" was written in discreet, spare lettering. The back of the clipboard he was holding had a white sticker on it with two purple male symbols and the words "Skylight Gay Night."

The couples all turned to look at me as I stepped out, but the bear looked completely unconcerned. He nearly filled the doorway, a mountain of white with a red handkerchief in his breast pocket. I wondered if that meant he liked watching other people have sex, or something.

I walked right up to him, and then I got his attention. "Name," he rumbled. I told him, and he checked the clipboard. There was no velvet barrier; apparently his authority was enough to keep people from charging through into the lounge.

The couples glared at me and I smiled back, trying to keep my tail from either wagging or curling. After a moment, the bear said, "Go on in."

Behind me, I heard one of the girls say, "Who's *he*?" but I ignored her. Maybe on Gay Night you shouldn't come as a straight couple.

Beyond a certain point, the scent of a crowd just becomes an indistinct mass, plus the two or three people closest to you with the strongest scents, but the twenty or thirty people in the Skylight hadn't brought the air to that critical mass yet. I could pick out the three females at the table to my right: two does and a mare. I could pick out the male wolf, the female ringtail, and the male skunk at the bar.

I strolled around the polished wood tables, nodded to the grey fox behind the bar, unsure if he was Jeremy's friend or not, and made my way to the other side of the bar, where a door opened out onto another patio. Whereas the one near the elevators seemed intended as a waiting area for people not yet in the club, this patio formed part of the club. The only thing they had in common was the ornamental hedge surrounding the space. A parquet floor covered the center of this patio, and at the far end, just in front of the hedge, a DJ table glowed faintly in the evening light. More cocktail tables stood around the edges, and here the colored lights that shone muted inside the bar glowed at full strength, illuminating the floor, the hedges, and two sculptures of leaping dolphins. The DJ stand was as empty as the rest of the patio, so I closed the door and went back inside.

A number of plush chairs sat empty around low tables. I curled my tail to the side and sat in one, and within moments, a rabbit in a tight white dress came to take my order. I got a martini because it felt like a classy thing to do, and sat there looking around at the other patrons. Everyone else sat casually draped over barstools, leaning on tables, smiling. Ears perked, tails swished, paws held drinks with a careless air. Gold and platinum credit cards flashed, and I saw smiles of recognition, waves, animated hellos and whispered pointing conversation. Only none of it was directed at me. I sat early, alone, and out of my element, no matter how much I looked the part.

Two overpriced but pretty darn good martinis and an hour and a half later, I sat in the same chair. The club had reached the "mass of scent" point now, with probably eighty people in the enclosed space. Not ten minutes ago, music had started outside, but people hadn't yet started filtering out there. I had been watching everyone come in, and had only spotted four red foxes: one female-female couple, one lone vixen, and a male fox too short and not fashionable enough to be Cristal. Jeremy had said I would know him when I saw him, so I had to assume he had not yet arrived.

In the meantime, I had moved very slightly toward feeling like I belonged there, mostly because I'd arrived before most of the people currently drinking and talking and touching. One guy, a coyote in a blue-purple satiny shirt, had sat down and made some conversation with me before getting distracted, or else feeling like I wasn't his type. If I hadn't been so intent on the door, I might have done better, but then again, I don't know much about the theater at the best of times, so his opening gambit of asking if I'd seen the new play "Little Lambs" wouldn't have done him much good.

I'd made idle conversation with two or three other people, and it served to remind me that although Cristal was my main objective here, he didn't have to be my only one. I could meet someone and make a date for later, or hell, if I met someone really interesting, I could dump Cristal right there and just go off with him. That led me to look around the bar and see who might be of interest.

The short red fox who wasn't Cristal still stood at the bar, apparently not with anyone. The coyote in the satin shirt was talking to a tall horse; I filed the horse away in my mind in case he ended up single later. I didn't know many horses, but I knew the stories people told about their equipment.

The only other guy in the bar who wasn't engaged in conversation was a sleek, elegant mink in a deep purple jacket and bright yellow shirt. He had come with a mixed group of about seven and had been laughing and talking with all of them for the past twenty minutes. Now the other six had resolved into three couples, leaving him alone as they filtered out to the dance floor, starting a small exodus. I stood to join them, because even my uncertain dancing would be better (or at the very least cheaper) than just sitting in the chair for another hour and having a third martini. There weren't that many foxes in the club, and I could come back periodically to check for Cristal.

The loud, pulsing beat came through the door and then exploded over me as I stepped out into the open-air dance floor. Without walls, the sound didn't get that headache-inducing reverberation that happens in loud enclosed spaces, but the speakers all pointed inward and the noise of the city filled in the empty spaces, and laughing people yelling to be heard generated yet another layer of sound.

But through it all cut the beat, mashed up with a rock song from my childhood. I took that as an omen and walked out to the dance floor. Swing and ballroom dancing follow a formal structure, but this was loose, casual, free. People swung their tails and shook their heads, kept arms by their sides or flung them out, did the back-and-forth step or got creative with their feet. The more energetic dancers gravitated to the center, whirls of graceful activity, while out on the fringes remained those who were less transported by the music, shifting in an easy, unchallenging rhythm.

The drinks had given me a pleasant low-level buzz, enough to let me start there on the edge, standing near some back-and-forthers. Gradually, as the music went on, I let myself go.

If the outer edge was the crust, and the hardcore dancers the core, then after two songs I found myself firmly in the mantle. My tail swept back and forth and I moved fluidly, but not too fast—faster than continental drift, though. The outside air had cooled only a little, but I was doing okay, not really noticing the warmth. When I'd gone dancing with Steven, what I'd really liked about it was losing myself in the rhythm, and I found myself using steps from our swing lessons.

I stopped in the middle of a song. Shit. I'd danced with that fox at the party. I was remembering that now. There'd been music going on, and I'd grabbed his paw and he'd swung me around, and I'd said something about "I don't know what I'm doing," and he'd said, "you're doing okay."

Slowly, I started moving to the music again, chewing over the memory, but before I could get into it, a paw touched my side. I looked down into the sharp muzzle of the mink in the purple suit. He grinned up at me and yelled over the music. "You doing okay? Ya went all funny there."

"Yeah," I said slowly. "Thanks."

He was still jog-dancing, so I started dancing again too. He had good moves, a lithe frame and a sense of rhythm, and he liked to slap his paws together to the beat. His purple jacket, lighter and looser than mine, billowed and flowed around him.

He stayed near me, and it felt like he was gauging my interest. So I said, "I like your dancing."

He grinned, shook his little tail, and kept going. For the rest of that song I thought I'd misjudged him, but when it rolled into the next, he turned back to me. "Hey, I gotta ask," he said. "Never seen a blue-checked handkerchief. What's it mean?"

"What?"

He gestured at my tail, and then I remembered. "Oh, shit," I said.

"That's brown, ain't it?" His teeth reflected all the colors flashing around us.

"No no, not that! Fuck. I'm sorry! I mean, it's, uh…" I eyed him. "You know, maybe I should get your name first."

"Geoff," he said, pronouncing it "Joff."

"I'm Lonnie."

"So?" He eyed my rear.

"Um. It's pretty generic, actually." I panted, and then caught myself, closing my muzzle.

He laughed and spun around to the music. "It's okay," he said. "I'm just wonderin', is all. Ain't seen you here before. Nice jacket."

"Thanks." I panted again. "It's warm, though."

"Head inside for a drink?"

We went back into the air conditioning, where the noise was slightly more muted, and after ordering drinks, I asked if Geoff knew Cristal. "Oh, sure," he said. "He's a regular here on Gay Nights. You looking for him?"

"Sort of." I didn't want to describe my whole mission.

"He usually rolls in around eleven with his posse."

My heart sank. "He has a posse?"

"One to three friends depending on the night." The mink sized me up. "You might could get his attention. New muzzle in the club and all that." He sipped his drink with a detached air that communicated his disappointment.

I kicked myself—literally, under the table. Here was a guy who was interested in me and I had just asked him about another guy. Way to go, Lonnie. "I only need to talk to him," I said, "but that's not for forty-five minutes, and he'll be here a while, so I've got lots of time."

Clumsy as it was, that renewed Geoff's interest. He told me a little about himself—he was a musician who'd just put out his second album and had seen good sales from it. I'd never heard of him, which disappointed him, but he gave me a business card and asked me about myself. Again, I felt like an impostor, dressed in a costume to meet someone who wouldn't give me the time of day otherwise. So I just told him I worked with the government, and when he pressed, I admitted I worked with the Geological Survey.

"Must pay pretty good," he said, and then lost interest in that part of the conversation. By this time, he was resting a paw on my thigh, and though it had felt weird at first, I'd gotten used to it, even started enjoying it. When we talked, our muzzles had to be pretty close in order to hear each other, and his breath was sweet from the drinks he'd had. When he started to trail claws down my pants leg, my tail wagged in response.

"Hey," he said, "you want, I can show you something."

The implied confidence overcame my awkward pretense. "Oh yeah?" I said. "Is it something you'd get in trouble for showing me in public?"

He chuckled, and his claws teased up closer to my crotch. "Might could be."

I reached for my phone to check the time and found my empty pocket. "Um…"

"Don't worry, I'll get ya back plenty of time to say hi to Cristal."

The bar was crowded. I checked around one more time to make sure there were no tall red foxes there, and then I daringly reached over and rested a paw on Geoff's thigh. His pants were so thin I could feel the warmth of his body through them, heat and firm muscle. "Sure," I said.

He chuckled, tossed a fifty onto the bar, and led me back out onto the dance floor. For a minute, pushed into the throng of people, I thought he was going to whip it out right there. It's an illusion in movies that you can do shit in a crowd of people and not be noticed. In a real crowd, people are looking around, not studiously away from the camera. You pull your pants down in a crowd, someone's going to look down and say, "Hey, not cool!" or something perhaps harsher.

I didn't get the chance to find out, because Geoff pulled me back toward the hedge that ringed the floor. We stood there at the edge as though we were taking a breather, and then I turned and he was gone.

My first thought was that this was all a joke. Then I heard a hiss, about the only sound I could've heard over the thumping, driving speakers, and I turned to see his dark head peering out from behind the hedge. He said something, but I couldn't catch any of the words, so I hurried over and squeezed through the small space between the blaring speaker and the end of the hedge.

The hedge did not go all the way to the edge of the roof, it turned out. There was a one-and-a-half foot wide path there, with tar paper laid down in sheets. Behind the hedge, the music was muffled and the scents muted. The sounds of the city drifted up faintly from below. I rested on the marble balustrade and looked out over the lights and cars. Jeremy had said he'd wait for me. I wondered if he were looking up at the roof.

A paw settled on my rear. "Nice an' private back here," Geoff said. "Ya check before ya come back, see if anyone's usin' it. Charisse Charmontaine showed me it."

"Who's that?" I swished my tail over his paw.

He grinned and pointed. "Right over there."

I followed his paw to a small billboard for a department store that featured an elegant pronghorn in a red dress. "You mean you saw the billboard, and…"

His paw got more gropey, squeezing and then teasing the underside of my tail, which got some more blood pumping to my sheath. "Nah, she was here at the club. We came back here and I got to see her tits."

"So," between the alcohol and the teasing and groping, my head was spinning a little, "you go both ways?"

"Depends on my mood," he said, and then in an exaggerated snobby manner, "My appreciation is for the varied beauty of any form."

He was certainly appreciating my form. I turned, because when someone's got his paw around the base of your tail and is working it into your waistband, it's polite to look them in the eye. But I only spent half a second looking him in the eye, because the paw that wasn't groping my butt was getting his pants open and pulling out a dark brown sheath and a warm reddish cock.

Well, what does one do after that? Two choices, I guess, and as he was already occupying himself with my pants, I opted for the second. He trailed his paw up his cock invitingly and then let it go, so I reached out and took hold of it.

It was warm and firm, and as I touched it I got a whiff of his musky scent. He closed his eyes and took a step closer to me. "So you know," he said, "we don't need to finish or nothin'. Just want to get to know each other a li'l better."

And with that, his paws were at the front of my pants, deftly undoing the belt and sliding inside to feel his way along my own warm hardness, which was definitely out of its sheath by that point.

"You don't want to come?" I asked.

He snorted, eyes closed at my touch. "Fuck up my threads? Go back out there smellin' like spit or jizz or whatever? Nah man, I'm good."

Okay, neither Derek nor Jeremy had prepared me for someone who'd want to hold my cock—and stroke along it, exploring it and teasing the tip enough to make me squirm—but not want to close the deal. The more I thought about it, though, the more it made sense. I mean, going back to McMinaver's and my hazy drunken "don't fuck in a place without a bathroom" rule. And anyway, I had Cristal to have sex with later, if everything went well. "Okay," I said. "And, uh, if you like it, we could meet up later."

"Sure," he said, leaning into me, and then he worked my cock out into the air, close to his so they were almost touching. Over his shoulder, I could see the "entrance" to our little private walkway, but we were so close that anyone poking their head around would just see two guys leaning together, no exposed flesh. That emboldened me, so I leaned over and rested my muzzle near his ear, exhaling across the fur.

He jerked a little, but didn't object, just kept caressing me, murmuring now and then: "You hot," or "leakin' out a bit," when his paw smeared something across my tip. He was leaky too, but didn't seem to mind that; the smell wasn't as strong as a full load by a long shot. And it was fun, just standing there with my nose in his fur, the lights of the city and the warm late spring air and the sounds of the party life behind us and the other life spread out below us, just dragging my fingers lazily up and down him, intimately, reaching down to tease his balls, feeling the fur of his sheath, pushing it down. My own need was growing slowly but not urgently, not pushing toward a climax as I was used to, and his fingers with their light touch and light, blunt claws felt like dancing sparks along my length.

"C'mon, wolf," he said. "Wanna see that knot. Here it comes. Here it comes." He squeezed at my base, getting a full-body squirm and laugh out of me as my tail wagged.

"If we don't finish," I murmured, "how do we know when we're done?"

"Aw, we done when we done," he said, reaching down to slide his paw under my sac and then farther back, getting claws almost under my tail before dragging them forward again through the fur and up around the base of my shaft, where my knot was pushing out. "That's nice," he murmured.

His shaft was thinner than the few I was used to, and, I thought, warmer. I wondered what it would feel like sliding into me, and then couldn't get that thought out of my head. Would it really be so dangerous to do it out here? Five minutes, probably; he could slip on a condom and fuck me while I leaned out over the railing.

"Nice big knot," he said into my chest, rubbing his nose against my bowtie.

Yeah, with me thinking about getting fucked, it probably was. I took a breath and tried to relax.

"Hey," he said, sharp and less dreamy, "not so hard. You wanna get me off?"

I had been stroking more firmly; I stopped now, trying not to project my own need onto him. So he really didn't want to come; it hadn't been just a line.

He stepped back, and I let go of him. "Sorry," I started to say, but he had his phone out, aimed at my crotch. "Wh—?"

"Sweet," he said, and a moment later there was a flash. He examined his phone. "Aw, yeah, came out real nice. Look at that knot." He turned the phone around.

Yep, sure enough, there was a picture of my cock, reddish-pink, harshly lit by the camera's flash, with the knot swollen at the base of it. "Uh."

"Don't worry." He tucked the phone away and reached over to tease the back of his fingers up and down my shaft again. "Just for me to remember. You wanna take a pic of mine?"

"Lost my phone. New one's on order 'til Monday." When I didn't take hold of him again, he reached for my paw and put it on his cock. I resumed stroking, and looked out at the billboard. "Did you take a picture of her tits, too?"

"Hell yeah." He snorted and then looked up at me, eyes sparkling with reflected city lights. "I got a whole collection. Show ya sometime."

After that, we didn't talk for long. I tried to relax and enjoy the feel of his cock, and he was definitely doing the same with mine. Despite my worries, we got to a point about ten minutes later when my mind started to wander, and his did too, and we both sort of looked at each other and took our paws back. As we stuffed our still-hard shafts back into our pants, he said, "Glad y'understand. Couple guys don't wanna take their junk out if they're not gonna blow a load."

"Well, I'm new at this," I said, and tried to ignore the leaking against the inside of my shorts.

He patted my butt. "You ain't new at it," he said. "Been practicing your whole life, ain'tcha?"

"I guess so." I got myself presentable again—mostly—and leaned on the balustrade, looking out. "Nah, this was fun." I knew I'd remember the warm intimacy of the encounter, even without a photo to help. I almost didn't want to go back out to the party, because back here, it didn't matter if I wore someone else's clothes. The photo had been weird, but perversely it made me feel better because it was of me. Geoff might have initially been attracted to me because of the clothes Jeremy'd picked out, but he'd brought me back here because of me and he'd spent a good twenty minutes or so stroking my cock because of, well, I guess he had a thing for canids, or maybe he just liked the, what did he say, "beautiful variety of nature." Either way, it was more fundamentally me than the clothes I'd hung on myself, no matter how good I looked in them.

Jeremy would be proud of me—maybe—when I told him. I felt a little slutty, but in a good way, and heck, maybe Geoff would want to get together again in the future. I wasn't sure what a musician would want to hang out with me for, but at least I was getting out and meeting people.

"A'right," Geoff said, and raised a paw. "See ya 'round."

Before I could say anything, he'd slipped along the walkway, quick and lithe, and had disappeared beyond the hedge. I took two steps and then stopped myself. Maybe it wouldn't look good if both of us came out together.

Two minutes later, I pushed my way back out onto the dance floor. Geoff was nowhere in sight, nor was he in the club proper, but as soon as I went through the doors, I forgot about him. Because standing right in front of me, leaning against the bar, was a tall, slender red fox with a bushy red tail that swished with a calm, even motion. The fox wore a dark fuschia jacket that curved down his back and flared out over his tail, and standing in profile to me, I could see the row of glittering studs down his ear and the light shirt—pink or salmon maybe—he wore under the jacket.

But it wasn't just his sharp profile, his tall black ears, or his fashion-magazine ensemble that made him stand out. He commanded the attention of the small crowd around him, eyes and ears turned up to him from all angles, and he bestowed his attention upon his court with a warm smile.

I took two steps in, wanting to get close to him too, and then thought, *how the hell am I going to manage that?*

There was no doubt that this was Cristal. Maybe when he came to McMinaver's he didn't have his posse, or maybe he just came to the party to…to something, get an easy lay, maybe, who knew. From what Derek had told me, everyone who was even remotely connected to the gay community came to McMinaver's; it could be as simple as that.

My first instinct was to say that Cristal clearly wasn't the fox who'd fucked me at the party. I mean, look at him. I couldn't imagine having forgotten that. Besides which, from the side he looked too thin. Well, thinner than I sort of vaguely remembered.

But what if it had been him? What if the clothes were slimming, what if he'd been dressed down, what if my rum-addled memory was not jiving with my somewhat gin-addled perception?

More to the point, I'd just spent twenty minutes stroking the cock of a successful musician I'd only just met. Who said I couldn't at least get some attention from this fashionplate fox?

Yeah, maybe it was just the three martinis talking—enough to stop me from walking out the door, not enough to embolden me to march right up to him. I worked my way to the bar nearby and perked my ears to listen to what he was talking about.

It was boring, to be perfectly honest. He was talking about some trip he'd taken overseas and peppering his travelog with quotations from various people whose names I didn't recognize, but which drew gasps from the listeners. Wait. One of those names was Charles Perrault, the name on the store Jeremy'd taken me to.

Really? He'd been palling around with a guy who had his own line of clothing stores? I turned to look at Cristal with a little more interest. Jeremy hadn't mentioned what he did, only what he was: a high-class snobby fox who slummed it in Cottage Hill. But it sounded like he was plugged in to fashion, and now I understood a little more why Jeremy had taken me to that store to dress me up.

Fortunately, I'd stationed myself at the left side of the bar, so when I faced forward, my right pocket, the handkerchief pocket, faced Cristal. I kept my ears perked in his direction, listening for an opening, but wow, that fox liked the sound of his voice.

Finally, after I'd sipped through most of my fourth martini, Cristal excused himself to use the restroom. I'd been there three times and knew the way well. I dropped my last twenty on the table with the same casual motion I'd seen Geoff use, waited a few minutes, and then sauntered toward the restroom, taking my time.

Sure enough, as I worked my way intentionally slowly around a table, the tall fox and his fuschia jacket emerged. And even in the crowd

of the bar, a light, sharp scent surrounded him, musky and cool like peppermint. I put myself in his path and put a paw out, then looked up and said, "Hey…"

He walked right on by.

I stood for a moment and then scrambled around a big brown rat to touch the fox's arm. "Cristal?"

He pulled his arm back as if I'd thrown up on it and looked down his considerably long muzzle at me. The studs in his ears sparkled and his nostrils flared. "Yes?"

"McMinaver's party," I said. "I…remember you."

I tried somehow to half-turn so my right-hand back pocket with the handkerchief would be visible, but my tail flipped around as I did and brushed the rat, who turned with some annoyance. I edged away and looked up. Cristal was still studying me, his mouth curved in distaste. "Cristal does not remember you," he said, his voice dripping with the effort it took him to acknowledge me, but the distaste faded from his muzzle as he took in my shirt. He took one more step toward the bar and then stopped, and his voice lost some of its pretension. "That jacket, though. Cristal would not have forgotten that."

"Oh, well," I said, "I didn't wear *this* to that party."

I tried to mimic his offhand condescension as best I could without starting to talk about myself in the third person (seriously, who *does* that?), and it only occurred to me after I'd said it that he might think I was mocking him. But someone has to be aware of his faults to pick up on being mocked, and Cristal just took my tone in stride. "Of course not," he said absently. "What was your name again?"

"Lonnie." I wanted to come up with a pretentious pronunciation of it, but I couldn't do it on the fly.

He shook his head, still staring at the jacket. "The name is not familiar."

"I know I'm not as memorable as you." He liked that. I could almost see him puffing himself up. "I'm working on it."

"The clothes are a good start," he said, and turned to edge past me.

"Want to dance?" I hurried it, because once he was back at the bar, I wouldn't get to him again for another half hour at least. Also because I was imagining that lean body next to mine, those elegant paws on my sides, and I was a bit turned on.

His lip curled again, and he looked out at the floor. "Cristal does not dance in places like this."

So he almost definitely wasn't my fox. Almost definitely. But he was close, and I wanted to give it my best shot. Anyway, to be honest, I'd sort of given up on having sex with him—he would never stoop to that, I figured—and was just having fun messing with him now. So I turned too, away from the dance floor, brushing my tail past his thighs so he'd look down and see the handkerchief. "Where would you like to dance?"

I tried to put air quotes around "dance," and wasn't sure if I'd succeeded. What I did feel was that I'd gotten a little bit higher than his thigh with my turn. He recoiled, and I waited for the blow-off, but he didn't move.

Over my shoulder, I checked him out and waited, completely lost in this part I was playing. He looked at the bar and then back at me, and then he just walked back to the bar.

Oh, well. Easy come, easy go. I'd certainly have a story to tell Jeremy when I got back downstairs, or whenever I saw him again. It had been fun, but it was also about time I left, so it was with very little regret that I made my way to the exit and the elevator. The bouncer moved aside for me, and the entire hallway, now crowded with people waiting to get in, turned envious eyes on me.

An arctic wolf in a sleek purple dress left the bar behind me, and the eyes turned to her as she sashayed over to stand next to me. We took the next elevator down to the lobby, in silence all forty floors down, and when the doors opened, I gestured gallantly for her to exit first.

She did, and then when I followed, she reached out and took my elbow. "Sorry," I said. "Did I—"

I broke off when I saw the guest elevators open, and the wolf pulled me into one. Having left the bar, my improvisation abandoned me. "Oh, I'm—look, where are we—what's going on?"

She didn't say anything, just put a finger to her muzzle and smiled at me. So that was interesting and mysterious and—exciting? I supposed? I mean, she didn't excite me the way that Cristal had, honestly, but it was exciting enough to have a mysterious beautiful stranger of either gender pull you into a hotel elevator. I'd seen enough spy movies. I wasn't made of stone.

Also I was still slightly buzzed.

So I rode up to twenty-two with her in silence, followed her to 2207, followed her inside, and then turned around as she backed out the door, the smile still on her muzzle. "Wait here," she said, and then the door closed.

Still exciting, I supposed. I sat on the bed, a fancy affair with about a dozen decorative pillows, blue and gold, and a satin bedspread that my tail hissed over as it swished. The rest of the room, too, fit my imagined standard for a luxury hotel. Blue wallpaper with a light gold pattern, paintings of beaches and boats, a cherry wood dresser and sixty-inch television, a white ceramic glow from a slightly ajar bathroom door (with gold handle), and a thickly plush carpet. The window looked out onto a patio, beyond which lay the same busy Port City I'd seen with Geoff from the roof. In here, the noise was muted, though my ears caught it even through the window.

The scent of the room was what was really impressive. It smelled like—nothing. It was almost creepy. I inhaled, inhaled again, and then walked to the bathroom just to get the flowery scent of the soap.

I'd just walked back to the bed and checked the bedside clock, wondering how long I'd have to wait, when the door lock clicked, and Cristal walked in.

He drew my eyes, and not just because he was walking into the bedroom with a swish to his tail, closing the door with a confident thunk. I straightened my back when I saw him, and the rest of the room dimmed as Cristal strode across the carpet, past the paintings, in front of the TV to stand in front of me on the bed.

His jacket was shed, folded, and set on the dresser in the blink of an eye, along with a small pillbox. I started to stand, paws going to my jacket's lapels, but the fox pushed down on my shoulders. "Stay down," he said, and slid his paws under the jacket's lapels, lifting it off. In a second, he'd folded it and set it next to his. I caught a whiff of some exotic spice, too light for me to have smelled in the club upstairs, that complemented his natural musk. If we hadn't been undressing and also smelling of our arousal, I would've happily just inhaled and sorted through all the layers of scent on him.

"Now the shirt," he said, and I started unbuttoning it while he worked his claws at the bowtie.

"A tied bowtie," he murmured. "Impressive."

He wasn't wearing a tie himself. His neck was right in front of my nose, and I could see the fluff of fur at the hollow of his collarbone. I exhaled there softly, drawing a chuckle from him. "Cristal must move this along quickly." His voice purred in my ears. "You don't mind?"

"No," I said, though it had barely been a question. "I'm just glad you came down—I mean, brought me to this room—or, had that wolf bring me."

Things had gone better with Porton when I shut up, so I clenched my teeth together. "Cristal will make sure you have an experience to remember," the fox said, either impervious to or unaware of my awkwardness. He pulled the bowtie free, letting it fall away as I unbuttoned the last button of my shirt.

While I leaned back, bare-chested, and unbuttoned my pants, the lean red fox straightened and opened the front of his shirt with a series of smooth flicks of his fingers. His chest, to my surprise, was not as attractive as Porton's. The other red fox had been a little plump, but Cristal was positively emaciated. The lean look worked under clothes, but as he shrugged his shirt off and pushed his pants down, he reminded me of a stick figure given fur.

That fur, though…wow. It gleamed in the light, rippled with color as he turned to fold our two shirts and his pants. Just by looking, I could tell it was as soft as the carpet. I'd thought his tail was impressive, but whatever he was doing with his tail, he did all over his body. And his black paw now lingered at his sheath, where his shaft was poking out and growing longer as I watched.

From the dresser, the paw that wasn't stroking his cock picked up the pillbox and extracted a small bottle of lube. "Back or stomach?" he asked me conversationally, now quite hard. His eyes on me were interested but polite, not eager.

"Um. No preference." I pushed my pants down mid-thigh, then lifted my left leg to get them the rest of the way off. The boxers came too, letting my shaft spring out into the room. It was still a little sticky from the fondling session with Geoff, and I saw Cristal's nostrils flare and his smile broaden. Probably thought I'd gotten all leaky just anticipating him sticking his golden tool in me. If it made him happier, I didn't mind.

When I'd kicked the pants off—apparently my pants didn't merit folding, or else he was getting a little more eager, because he left them on the floor in a heap—he leaned over me and took my shaft in his paw. I reached up to touch his arm, and good lord above, his fur was even softer than it looked, somehow. I couldn't stop running my fingers over it. The light spicy scent I'd caught on him wasn't in the clothes; it was in his fur.

He leaned farther over, allowing me to slide my fingers down his side as I lay back on the bed, legs and tail still hanging over the edge. I was expecting to feel bone, but the soft fur more than made up for the leanness of his form. His ribs tripped below my fingers, and then I came down into the curve of his abdomen to the jutting bone of his hip. All the while, his paw stroked me with urgently, more roughly than Geoff's had.

The combination of exploring his lean body, watching his shaft bob in front of me, and his paw pumping my own erection was having an effect, especially coming so closely on the heels of Geoff's teasing. Squirming and tense, I moved my fingers to his tight, hard stomach, and then the tighter hardness below it.

"Your—Cristal's fur is exquisite," I panted, and then couldn't keep a small whine out of my throat.

He just smiled, watching keenly as I shivered below him. His paw kept moving, that even, steady rhythm tightening my balls and shortening my breath. My tail wagged below me and I spread my legs, then closed them around his slender, muscled thighs as he leaned in.

And still he kept going. Shit, was he just going to jerk me off into my stomach? I sucked air through my nose and pulled my fingers along his shaft, trying to catch him up to me, but the only sign of his arousal was a little leaking along my fingers. "I—huh—" I gasped, trying to warn him of the surge cresting in my groin.

He stopped and smiled down at my slow descent from almost-climax. When he stepped back, his cock slid out of my fingers, and I panted, lying back on the bed as he reached for the lube and shot a burst into his paw. Almost immediately, those slick fingers were pushing under my tail, working around and in, and I had to bite my lip again. I lifted my legs to allow him better access, and put my paw over my muzzle to muffle my whines.

The fingers came out and I kept my legs up, breathing heavily. And then I got a shock. I could smell his pre on my fingers, strongly enough now that they were away from his exotic scented fur. And the scent was—was it the same? My head was muddled with sex and booze and spice, but if it wasn't the same as my mystery fox, it was pretty damn close.

That would explain why he'd just left quietly, and while he might not remember me specifically, he seemed like the type who wouldn't let random sexual encounters stick very long in his mind. Well, it wasn't going to be a romantic story, maybe—I doubted I'd see him again unless I went way out of my way to do it—but it was nice to know who it had been. Now I could get on with my—

"Uh. Hey. Cristal."

I hadn't really been paying attention to what he was doing, distracted by the scent, but I'd noticed him slicking up his cock, and until he lowered himself and placed it at my rear, I hadn't registered that

I hadn't seen him open a condom. His grey eyes looked placidly down at me, eyebrow arched.

"Um. You have a condom on, right?" I couldn't really see over the mound of my stomach and the pinkness of my own erection.

"Not to worry," he said. "Cristal will not catch anything from you."

"That's—that's not—"

His gaze turned dark, and his nose lowered toward mine. "You insinuate that *Cristal* has a disease? How dare you?"

"No, no! Whoa. It's just good sense."

"You are with Cristal now. There is no need for…"

"Oh, whoa, hey." He'd started to push into me, and as much as I hated doing it, I scooted back on the bed. "I'm sorry. You're gorgeous and all, but I don't—not without a condom—my mother made me promise—" Mom *actually* made me promise never to talk to her about my sex life, but she also, before I was gay, made me promise to always use a condom.

He stepped back, need and scorn warring in his expression, one lip twisted up to show his canine tooth on that side. It wasn't a good look. "Your *mother?*"

He might just walk out of the room, I realized. I could just say that the scent was close enough and that Cristal had slummed it with me at McMinaver's—only the fox there had used a condom, and I didn't remember having to insist, and what's more, even though the smell was close, I didn't *want* it to be him.

"Please don't go," I said, at first trying not to beg and then figuring that he was probably good with the idea of people begging him for sex. "It's not such a bad thing, is it?"

Those grey eyes glared at me from beneath a lowered brow. "Cristal is clean."

"Of course you are." He started to step forward again, his expression lightening. I raised a paw. "No, no, I mean, it's me. I'm just…"

The thin fox drew a finger along his length. "Do you want this, or not?"

I bit my lip. In addition to wanting to know, I did very much want that in me, mostly because I was all worked up. If my body were a democracy, the majority would definitely have ruled to wave Cristal forward and get fucked—after all, he probably was clean. But my brain was still in charge of my mouth, and so over the protestations of my aching shaft and tense muscles, I said, "I do—I do very much. But…I can't…" I swallowed. "If you wanna jerk off on my stomach, sure, but… look, I've got one in my wallet…"

Cristal stared at me for a moment. Then he growled and spun around, heading for the dresser where he'd laid his clothes, and I thought he was going to walk out. But he picked up the pillbox, thumbed it open, and pulled a condom out of it. So he'd had one all along, the bastard. If I weren't all lubed up and all worked up…well, no, let's face it, I wasn't about to walk out the door in any case.

He didn't look me in the eye as he rolled the condom on, nor as he situated himself and pushed into me. He didn't take hold of my shaft, and his thrusts came quick and abrupt, burying himself in me all the way and then pulling back out. I took my cock in my own paw and closed my eyes. He still smelled exotic and he still felt great going into me, and I thought, yeah, familiar. Yeah, he's the one from the party, sliding in like that, although then he'd been less angry, more mellow, and the thrusts had been easier, and…

His hips slammed against my rear. "Huh…huh…huh…" I panted, but Cristal didn't make a sound. It was perhaps the least intimate sex I'd ever had, but with my eyes closed and no sound from him, I could let my imagination wander, and that was enough for me.

The thrusts sped up, his paws lowered to the bed, he pounded into me over and over, and I felt the thickness of his knot against my rear. He pushed hard, and almost got the knot in, but pulled back at the last minute. And did it again. And then a short, soft whine escaped him, and his body went rigid, and then he yanked himself back and out and before I could tell myself to hold onto the memory of him, the paws on the bed lifted. A second later the bathroom door slammed, and the shower started running.

I finished myself with my paw, a nice little orgasm with his leftover warmth, and relaxed back on the bed. Here was a new experience for me: getting fucked by a complete douche. My legs relaxed off the side and my tail wagged anyway. All in all, douchery aside, it had been a pretty good fuck. I even—

There was something still in my rear. I hadn't felt it at first, but now, relaxing, it became obvious. I reached around there, giving my shaft another stroke on the way—kind of a 'nice job, buddy'—and poked cautiously at my entrance with a claw.

Oh, of course. Cristal had slicked up his cock and then put the condom on, and when he'd pulled himself out, the latex had stayed behind. Delicately, I extracted it, and held it up. It was full, so at least he hadn't leaked into me anywhere.

On my way to the trash to throw it away, I stopped. It wouldn't hurt to be sure…so I took a breath and then put my nose to the opening of the condom.

Thick, powerful musk assailed me. Still, it reminded me of Steven, just as my mystery fox had—but was it identical? Oh, hell. I took another long sniff, and then wondered if I could get a bit of it out onto a tissue to take with me. That felt either like I was a stalker or a spy. I settled on spy, and I will cut short the details of how I did it. Suffice to say that when Cristal emerged from the bathroom, clean and soft and still not looking at me, I had a bit of his scent that I could take back and compare.

He didn't say a word as I entered the bathroom. It was no surprise to me that when I finished my shower, he was gone.

CHAPTER SEVEN

At The Morning After, the…well, the morning after, I sat with Jeremy and drank a sweet milky coffee and ate pancakes, and told him with some relish about my night. He wore a filmy blue scarf and a sleek white linen shirt that hung loosely around his shoulders, and his claws were painted blue to match. He listened attentively, and seemed more surprised about Geoff than about Cristal. When I asked him about it, he just smiled.

"Well, you were dressed to appeal to Cristal. I like that you went for it with the mink, though. Well done."

"I just hope that some picture of my junk doesn't end up all over the Internet."

Jeremy laughed. "Oh, sweetie, who'd know? Only people who've seen it anyway, and probably not even most of those. Wolf cocks all look the same if you're not a wolf."

"That's not true," I said. "I've had three different fox cocks in the last week…and a day…and they've all been different."

"Yes, but could you tell them apart from a photo?"

"Probably?"

He lifted his mimosa glass and toasted me before sipping from it. "Well, to you—two in one night! And to the—what was the phrase? Infinite and beautiful variety of the male form."

"Close enough," I said, and I thought about Porton and Geoff, Cristal and my mystery fox. Four different guys—that was more than I'd had in the previous…rest of my life. "Actually, I like yours better."

He nodded in thanks and picked at his egg white omelet. "How do you feel?"

"Me? I feel okay. I mean, I had good foreplay and a good lay last night, and it doesn't matter that they weren't with the same person."

"I meant in general." He sipped, looking at me over the rim of his glass. "You broke up, moved house, new job, new friends…and now the world of casual sex."

I looked around. The Morning After wasn't crowded this morning, possibly because there hadn't been any big parties the previous night. But it was my second week in a row, and already I was looking forward to the next Sunday morning. "It's not the casual sex so much," I said. "It's… well, I don't expect to see Cristal or Porton again, but maybe I'd run into Geoff, but…I mean, I don't know…I feel better sitting here having breakfast with you than I did during all those times."

His white-lined eyebrows rose again. "Either there is something I don't know about the coffee here, or you've had a series of exceptionally disappointing sexual encounters."

The seriousness of his pronouncement and the sparkle in his eyes made me laugh. "I can have sex anywhere," I said.

"Really?"

"Well—I mean, on the roof of a hotel? In a stranger's bedroom?"

"Point taken." He inclined his head.

"But it's here," I went on, "with you and—and Derek—that I feel part of a…community. Like I belong."

"And that's what's important to you."

"I suppose so."

Jeremy lifted a paw and signaled to someone behind me. I half-turned and saw Gilliam, the ferret, coming toward us.

He pulled out a chair and sat down at the table. "Hallo, dear," Jeremy said. "Good morning?"

"Yes, I'm just meeting Martique and Victor," Gilliam said, "and maybe Sy. How are you two?" He looked at me and flared his nostrils, sniffing. "Lonnie, right? From McMinaver's?" He asked how I'd been, and Jeremy told him right off that I'd been trying to track down the fox I'd had sex with at the party. Gilliam smiled. "A Cinderella quest, eh?"

Jeremy laughed. "Yes. Getting some princes to try on the glass condom."

I flicked my ears, but they were both smiling. "Kind of, only…I don't want to run off and marry him when I find him."

"And what do you want?" The ferret showed no judgment, only casual interest.

"Well, I—I just want to know. Wouldn't it bother you if you'd had sex with someone and didn't know who it was?"

Gilliam tapped his whiskers. "Maybe? I don't know. I don't remember everyone I've had sex with, but I don't think it's that odd. Mind you, I hang out with Martique and Victor…"

"We'll introduce you." Jeremy leaned across the table. "They'd like you."

The ferret didn't seem quite as convinced, but he didn't argue. "Speaking of them, there they are." He pointed out the window.

"So," I said as he got up, "this 'glass condom' thing, that doesn't seem weird?"

Gilliam squinted at me. "When you've met Martique and Victor," he said, "you can decide if you want to ask me that question again. They've sort of recalibrated my scale of 'weird' when it comes to sexual things." He raised a paw. "Nice to see you again. Good luck with the glass condom."

"There you are," Jeremy said when he was gone. "He remembered you."

Gilliam brought Martique, a red fox (not tall enough to be *my* fox), and Victor, a pronghorn, over to our table. Martique hung over my shoulder and his tail brushed mine, and he and Victor asked several questions to try to help pinpoint my mystery fox, but they didn't come up with any names Jeremy hadn't already considered. They wished me luck, and as they left, Martique was saying to Victor, "We should do something fun like that sometime."

Jeremy and I wrapped up our conversations and paid, and sat there just talking about music and movies, and not much else. That's what we were doing when Derek walked in.

The rat saw him first. He waved again, as he had with Gilliam, and I half-turned again, and when I saw the big, muscular wolf standing awkwardly in the doorway in a tank top and shorts, I just stopped and looked at him. He was looking at me, too, waiting, and the echo of the previous day's conversation ran through my head. But it wasn't strong enough to overcome friendship, and so I waved him over.

He came reluctantly and I watched him all the way. When he pulled up the chair Gilliam had been sitting in, he didn't sit down right away. "I'm not interrupting, am I?"

"Please," Jeremy said. "Sit."

"Yeah," I said. "It's cool."

He fitted himself into the chair and sat, his tail just dangling down behind him without much motion. "Thanks. Lonnie, I actually came here to look for you to, uh, I saw Jeremy's ScentBook check-in here." When I didn't say anything, he went on, "How are you guys?"

We told him we were good, and then he turned to me. "How'd it go at the Twilight?"

I didn't correct him. "Oh, I got a little action. Jeremy dressed me up right and I generated, um." I took a sip of my coffee. "The right kind of interest."

"Good," Derek said. "So did you find your fox?"

"No, I'm afraid not."

He looked about to stop, and then he looked down and a little glint appeared in his eye. "But you eliminated one more suspect?"

I nodded. "He was close, but...when I compared directly, not quite."

"Well." He smiled, uncertain. "I guess that's good."

"I had a good time anyway." And because he was being nice, and I felt bad, and he'd clearly come here to try to smooth things over, I said, "I'll come to your bar next weekend, if you want. Sorry for being snappy yesterday."

"Oh, maybe."

Jeremy, who'd watched with a smug smile, said, "Well, we do have one more fox to check out. I was thinking next weekend, but it'll take a little while, of course."

Derek frowned. "Aren't you done? I mean, if it wasn't the first two, it must have been Wendell, right?"

I hadn't even thought of that. I turned to Jeremy, but he was smiling. "I guess..." I said. "If there weren't any other foxes..."

"There could have been one we didn't see." Jeremy held up four fingers on a paw and ticked off a name for each one. "Those four foxes might have been at the party."

Derek turned to me. "Still nobody responded to your post?"

"Two more offers of no-strings sex. That's it."

"So..." The big wolf folded his arms. "Why are you going to all this trouble to have sex with foxes who don't want to, when you have all these offers from foxes, or whoever, who do?"

I rubbed my muzzle. "I don't know. This is...more fun. I mean, it feels like I'm after something more than just sex."

Neither of them seemed to know what to say to that. Derek cleared his throat. "Isn't the last fox the married one?"

Jeremy and I looked at each other. "Yeah," I said.

"And what if he's the one? What are you going to do, become his..." Derek waved a paw. "Mistress? What's the word?"

"No," I said, though I'd asked myself that question and wasn't quite sure of the answer. "I just want to *know*."

"Uh-huh. And to find out, you're gonna get him to cheat on his husband?"

He said it with a meaningful look at me, and I have to admit that I hadn't thought that far ahead. But as it turned out, I hadn't needed to. "Oh," Jeremy broke in, "I have a plan for that."

*

His plan was pretty simple in concept, but it required me to do a couple things I'd never done well. The big one was flirting.

So Jeremy got the two of us invited to dinner at Taylor and Wendell's Wednesday night, and Tuesday evening he sat down with me to work on my flirting. I felt like I'd been shoved back into high school, where all around me my friends were pairing off and I would walk out of study halls and after-school bull sessions wondering why nobody had flirted with me. Only years later (when it was far too late) did a couple of my female classmates tell me they had been.

Coming out in college (just before college, technically) was something of a relief. That, I thought, was why I hadn't been able to flirt in high school. I wasn't straight; that was all. But the LGBT scene in college turned out the same. People paired off, grew closer and fell apart, and I understood the deeply hidden chemical processes that formed igneous rocks better than I understood the deeply hidden emotional processes that formed relationships. Steven had pursued me, appreciated my shyness, made everything easy. I had to assume my fox at the party had done the same.

It was only since I'd had a goal, something that drove me, that I was able to make daring moves like I had at the restaurant with Porton, or in the club with Cristal. Then it felt like a game, not like the start of a relationship. Games, those I understood.

So Jeremy worked on flirting with me. Over two hours, we worked on eye contact, subtle compliments, "accidental" touches, and by the time we'd finished, he pronounced me ready to go to dinner with a fox and civet. "Or," he said, "at least ready to go to dinner on a learner's permit. With a licensed driver accompanying you."

And so Wednesday night came around. I'd gotten my new phone and put most of my contacts back into it. I'd left another message for Steven telling him I had a new phone, but he hadn't replied. With Jeremy at my side, though, the sting of Steven's indifference faded, and I felt more confident facing the world—or at least facing a gay married couple.

I'd figured Porton to be a couple years older than me. Jeremy was probably in his late twenties, and Cristal probably late twenties or early thirties. Geoff—no idea. But Wendell and Taylor were in their mid-fifties, frosted with grey around their ears and muzzle, a little slower to move, but no less bright and smiling for all that.

Wendell looked like the most likely candidate for my mystery fox so far. He was just about six feet, a little pudgy around the middle like me, and he smelled floral and fresh. His clothes were stylish, if not Jeremy's kind of stylish; he wore a white button-down shirt with green pinstripes, which set off his hazel-green eyes. Taylor, his husband, was a chirpy little civet slightly shorter than me, and he did all the cooking. He appeared briefly to say hello, neck rings fluffed out over the collar of a designer t-shirt and dirty white apron, and then he retreated back to the kitchen while Wendell showed us into their living room and offered us wine.

I knew a little bit about wine, but not enough to be discerning, so I let Jeremy accept for both of us. The three of us sat and talked while Taylor called out commentary from the kitchen. As I was the new kid on the block, the main topic of conversation was me.

Wendell was gracious and polite, and interested in my geology degree. "I've always liked rocks," he said in a light baritone, his whiskers bouncing as he smiled.

"You used to date one," Taylor called from the kitchen, and we all chuckled.

"I'm a structural geologist." I explained at a high level the study of rock formations, of faults and microstructures.

"Do we have faults out here? I thought that was a West Coast thing."

"Some," I said, "but not serious ones. Faults are interesting because they're places where the structure changes violently, but only when the pressure there builds up to a point. You'd think you could tell when that point will be, but there are so many variables that it's hard to predict. Most rock formations change gradually over time on a more or less continuous scale, but faults give you beautiful jagged formations."

"Cool," he said. I asked about his job, and he talked some about his work as a director at a bank, which made me feel a little self-conscious. I mean, that was a job like one of my father's friends would've had, and here I was trying to be a peer to this guy—and more, maybe. I tried to envision him in the blue shirt, standing with a drink in one dark brown paw, grabbing me and dancing.

Taylor called from the kitchen. "He's terrific with money. He gives me all I need."

Wendell grinned fondly in that direction. "Taylor does organization and promotion for a non-profit gay and lesbian legal foundation. They helped bring marriage to the state."

"We got our picture in the newsletter!"

"It pays, but not all that well, so I chip in with some of his causes."

"Hon, can you c'mere a sec?"

Wendell said, "Excuse me," and rose, padding to the kitchen, where Taylor gave him something to taste. If it was anything like the smells coming from the kitchen, it must have been divine.

"I don't know if I can do this," I hissed to Jeremy. "It's like flirting with one of my dad's friends."

The rat blinked back at me. "So?"

One of my dad's friends, a big wolf named Mr. Haggerty, had cornered me when I was home from college for a picnic. He'd heard I was gay and very indelicately asked if I fooled around with older guys. I got away by telling him I heard his wife calling. That was the image in my head as I poked Jeremy. "Seriously."

"Seriously," he said. "He likes you. Don't worry about it."

And then Wendell was back, curling his long russet tail delicately around himself as he sat in the armchair, and we resumed our conversation until dinner was ready. I tried to forget any resemblance to Mr. Haggerty (there was very little; Wendell was cuter and way more confident) or anyone else, for that matter. Fortunately, Wendell made it easy. Grey ears or no, I really enjoyed talking to him, whether about my interests or his. I even forgot about trying to get him into bed.

Taylor was a terrific cook. He'd made stuffed mushroom appetizers, "with some ground pork because we're mostly all carnivores here," with a sly glance at Jeremy. They were delicious, and as I ate the first one, my stomach growled, and I ate two more before I caught Jeremy's eye and stopped, politely.

Then wine was poured around, and I had enough to get a little bit light-headed, and then Taylor brought out the salads, simple affairs with lettuce and radishes and croutons and a really nice light vinaigrette dressing. The radishes had been flowered, which Jeremy commented on and Wendell said Taylor had learned to do that years ago and couldn't resist showing it off, and Taylor just smiled and dipped his pointy muzzle.

The main course, a roast fowl with what Taylor described as a "plum and burgundy wine sauce," was also delicious, and even if Jeremy hadn't told me to compliment the food effusively, I would have. The side of potatoes au gratin with garlic, "a light touch for my fox's sensitive nose," and the fresh-baked bread—it was all amazing, and I said so often.

"I didn't know bread could taste this good," I said.

"Even in the northeast?" Taylor wanted to know, and so I told him about this one bakery a block away from the college, and how one year I lived close enough that I could open my window in the morning and smell the crisp, yeasty baking aroma.

"I didn't get bread there so often," I said. "More their sticky buns."

I said it without thinking, and there was a pause in the conversation. Nobody snickered, but I think everyone took my remark as innuendo. Jeremy gave me a covert smile, and we went on talking.

All the while, I was trying to use Jeremy's eye contact trick, and I thought it might be working, but I wasn't sure. It was hard, because I'd be trying to make eye contact with Wendell, and then I'd notice Taylor looking at me and I got all self-conscious, so then I tried to look at him, but then worried that I was neglecting Wendell. Anyway, I got only polite stares in return, although once I did think I saw the curve of a smile on the civet's muzzle, under the grey-frosted black mask.

We retreated to the living room again to rest before dinner. Taylor cleared plates and Jeremy said, "Let me help," and that left me alone with Wendell.

He'd plopped himself down in the armchair again, which momentarily stymied me. I'd planned to sit next to him. Maybe I should just give up, I thought. It was going to be awkward enough as it was, and I was full of good food and warm with wine. My tail wagged slowly without me even thinking about it, which it does when I'm content, and when I thought about flirting, I worried about ruining the nice feeling I was getting from this evening.

But then Jeremy called from the doorway to the dining room, "Lonnie, did you notice their oriental hanging?" That was the cloth with the gold dragon on it positioned, it so happened, right behind Wendell's chair.

When I walked over to look at it, the fox turned. "We got that on a trip to Hu-Xiong. Taylor bargained with the store owner for half an hour."

"It's gorgeous." I leaned close to sniff it and caught a scent of oriental spice, faint but still present. "I can still smell the city on it."

He was pleased by that, whiskers twitching on his long muzzle. "Taylor can't smell it anymore. He says I'm imagining it."

My heart beat fast. I took a breath and leaned back casually, resting my paw on the back of the chair, very close to Wendell's tall black ears. "It's definitely there," I said, and wished I could come up with a good segue or innuendo or something, but one thing Jeremy had stressed to me was that I should lay off the cheesy movie lines ("they seem desperate, sweetie"). So I just looked around the room and said, "I haven't been in a room this nice since McMinaver's."

His ears twitched at that, and he looked up at me. "Oh, you were there? It was a gorgeous party this time. Of course, he can afford a line of hula dancers and roast pork and those brass pineapple decorations."

"And the mojitos." I kept eye contact with him and let my tail wag.

"Mai tais are more my speed."

"The mojitos sort of got me into a s—situation." I'd just stopped myself from saying "sticky."

He looked genuinely concerned, his ears laying back. "Nothing serious, I hope."

"No, it was fun. I mean, it wasn't something I'd normally do, but I liked it a lot. I'm starting to open my horizons." I paused. "Jeremy says."

All the while, I was leaning in until my chest (and one of those fancy shirts I'd bought) was just a couple inches from his muzzle. He didn't recoil or anything, but he also didn't lean forward. "Coming out of your shell a bit? You mentioned a boyfriend."

"Ex-boyfriend." I was so close, it would've been easy just to reach over and brush his ears. And habit pulled at me to do just that, so I had to fight against it. Shoulders weren't as intimate as ears, though, so I trailed a paw over his shoulder as I walked back to the couch and sat down. "I guess I was sort of locked into the relationship. It was comfortable and easy."

He asked how it ended, and I told him about Steven and the lion, and in the middle of that, Jeremy came back out, followed soon by Taylor. We talked a little longer before Taylor got up and asked if we were ready for dessert.

Jeremy said, "Oh, you've made the whole dinner. Let me and Wendell get dessert ready."

"You're a guest," Taylor said, but Jeremy was already standing.

"I insist." The rat pushed Taylor back down to the couch—beside me—and beckoned Wendell. The red fox got up, a faintly bemused look on his muzzle, and followed Jeremy to the kitchen with a swishing of his tail.

I turned to the little civet, and he grinned at me. "So," he said, "you're as cute as Jeremy said you were."

My tail wagged, once. "You guys are, too. I mean, you're as great as Jeremy said."

"Glad you think so. Wendell's a dear and I really don't deserve him. But I do what I can to keep him happy, and that's worked for some years now."

"How many?"

"It was sixteen in March. Officially only married for two, of course."

"It must have been a lovely wedding." That wasn't flirty, it was sincere, based on who they were and how pretty the house was.

So he told me about their wedding, and in the process of telling, he leaned against me and pulled out his phone and started showing me photos. We were still doing that when Jeremy came back out.

"Well, don't you two look thick as thieves," he said with a smile. "Come on in and have some key lime pie."

And as he got up, Taylor braced himself with a paw on my thigh, and so I, daringly, brushed his lithe civet tail as I got up to follow. He half-turned, smiling, and I held his eyes, returning a smile and a wag.

The pie was tart and creamy, the whipped cream fresh and sweet, which at least partly explained what had taken them so long in the kitchen. If either Wendell or Taylor felt discomfited by my flirting, neither showed it. Taylor, in fact, had been flirting back with me, I was pretty sure.

I didn't get confirmation of that until we were saying good-bye, Jeremy and I both regretfully pleading work the next day. Wendell had remained in his armchair, but Taylor'd squeezed into the sofa between me and Jeremy, and we all felt like old friends, especially the time Taylor put a paw on my tail and left it there. And when we'd gotten up and were shaking paws, Wendell grasped mine and held my eyes with his, and said, "I hope it won't be too long until we see you again. Taylor really likes you."

Taylor swatted him but didn't deny it, and left a paw at the small of my back as Jeremy and I walked out. They called good nights, and when the door had closed and we were walking to Jeremy's car, the rat chuckled. "That seemed to go well," he said.

"They're both really sweet," I said. "Was I just supposed to flirt with Taylor to make it okay for me and Wendell to have sex?"

Jeremy laughed and unlocked his car. When we'd sat down and closed the doors, he said, "You really don't know?"

"Know what?" I shook my head.

He started the car. "If they like you, you won't be having sex just with Wendell."

CHAPTER EIGHT

A threesome with a married couple? What if I paid more attention to one than the other? What if one of them liked me and the other didn't? What if I embarrassed myself in front of both of them? I liked them enough that even if Wendell turned out not to be my mystery fox (and now I was hoping he wasn't, because I didn't want him to have cheated on Taylor) I didn't want to screw things up.

Thursday at work I ran to the bathroom to check my phone so often that Kevin asked if I'd eaten something bad the night before. But the only message I got was from Derek, asking me to dinner that night.

On the way there, I called Jeremy and babbled at him about my insecurities for a while. "Settle down," he said. "Taylor and Wendell have shared their bed before. I wouldn't have suggested this if you were going to be the first."

"Wendell didn't recognize me," I said, "even when I mentioned McMinaver's. So I don't think he's the one."

"Well, if you really don't want to do it," Jeremy said, "you only have to say no if they ask."

"After all that flirting I did?"

"Sweetie." His voice remained high and firm. "You don't have to do anything you don't want to. Tell them I was egging you on, if you like. But remember the flip side of that, too."

"Which is?"

"You *can* do anything you *do* want to."

"That's not strictly true," I argued. "What if I want to have sex just with Wendell? Or Taylor?"

"Do you?"

"That's—that's not the point." The thought of the threesome was actually tempting, really tempting, mostly because I'd never done it before. "The point is that me wanting something isn't enough. The other guy—guys—have to—has to—whatever, someone else also has to want it."

He was quiet for a minute, and then he said, "God, I forgot how terrifying it is to be right out of college."

"Oh, what does that have to do with anything?" I snapped.

"Lonnie, you're overthinking. Look, let's—how do you do this in geology? Reduce the problem to its simplest components. If Taylor and

Wendell want to have sex, they'll invite you over for a date, probably this weekend. I told them that you liked them both, in that way, in case they weren't clear on it, and so they know that if they want to reciprocate, the ball's in their court. So to speak. If, when they call, you decide you don't want to finish your quest, then you don't have to do it. They won't hold it against you, I promise."

I exhaled. "You make it sound so easy."

"It is easy, you adorable wolf. Look, you invited me into your bed—well, my bed, but you were in it—and I didn't want to accept. We're still friends, right?"

"Yes." I grudgingly lowered the dial on my freak-out-o-meter. "Wait. Why did you tell them that I liked them like that?"

"It was true, wasn't it?"

"Yes, I—that's not the point, though. I mean, why can't you tell me whether they like me or not?"

"Did you not pick up on their signals? They do like you."

"Then why couldn't they just pick up on my signals?"

He paused. "You're also ready to hop into bed. Or if you're not, you can decide that. They need time to think about it, decide if they want to do it. Their decision is a little more complicated and I just gave them a little more information to help them make it. In this case, sweetie, you have to let them take the initiative, but when—I think it will be 'when'—they issue the invitation, they'll understand that you have a decision to make, too. Does that help?"

"Maybe. I guess. Sort of."

"My dear wolf, I am rooting for you. I'm just trying to help."

"You're doing a lot to help me get laid," I said. "Not just setting all this up, but the club, the clothes…"

"You're my project for the spring. It does my heart good to live through you."

"Well. Glad I can help." My tail wagged even though I still wasn't a hundred percent satisfied. "I gotta go. I'm meeting Derek for dinner."

"Just remember," Jeremy said. "You can do whatever you want to."

I tried to keep that in mind as I sat down across from Derek at the Middle Eastern place down the street from my apartment. He got the kebabs, loading up on protein, while I got a wrap. We made small talk, and then he did that thing where he squares his shoulders and looks at me and then looks away, which lets me know that he's about to talk about something serious.

"So how'd this thing go? You picking up this married guy?"

"It was just dinner." I laid my ears back. Ordinarily I would've bragged to Derek about what I was getting set up for.

"Them? So you met the husband?" He waited, and then went on. "And that's it?"

"Maybe. I don't know."

The big wolf nodded and shoved a lump of meat into his muzzle, chewing. I didn't know if he was going to say anything else, and I was going to let the subject drop. But I remembered Jeremy saying I could do anything I wanted to, and dammit, I wanted an answer from him.

"Listen, what's going on with you?"

He flicked his ears back, and looked guardedly at me. "What do you mean?"

"Well, when I had sex at the party—the party *you* took me to—you were all like, 'way to go, bro!' And now you're telling me not to go to clubs, not to go flirt with Wendell…" The restaurant was small, but it didn't even occur to me to look around to see who might be listening. "What happened to the guy I sent pics of my balls to?"

That made him smile, and he said in a mock-pout, "You didn't send me pics from the other night."

"Well, let's see. The night with Porton I was with him until I got mugged. Then I didn't have my phone. But speaking of photos…" I told him about Geoff, and then about Cristal, concluding with, "So he was a douche, but you know, I did it. I'm getting out there. And I'm being safe. I made him use a condom."

He poked at the rice on his plate. "I guess that's kind of what's bothering me, maybe."

"What, that I'm having safe sex?"

"That you're having so much of it." He gave me a soft, brotherly smile that looked really touching on his big muzzle. "I really want you to be happy, Lonnie. I thought you were so sweet when you came out to me. You were shy, you were adorable, and you were the only guy who came out to me that year who didn't right away try to get me in bed. You just wanted to be friends, and that was cool. And you kept in touch when we moved away. When you and Steven moved in, I was really happy, and I kind of looked at you as being the role model for me. I could never find someone I was happy with in a relationship kind of sense. But I was glad you did. Then when Steven broke up with you, I wanted to fly up there and punch him."

"I'm glad you didn't."

"Really?" He raised his eyebrows. "He treated you like shit."

"No. He just—we changed, and he let me down easy, and we moved on…" I trailed off.

He leaned across the table. "He broke up with you the week before Valentine's Day."

I looked down at the table and mumbled, "He didn't want to go to Valentine's Day dinner with me, knowing he was going to…it was sparing my feelings."

"Bullshit. He took that lion out to Valentine's Day dinner, didn't he?"

I blinked. "I don't know."

Derek waved away the point. "He claimed he was changing and all this crap, but all that happened was he found someone else he wanted to fuck, and he went for it."

Steven wouldn't have gone to Valentine's Day dinner with Cranston. Not so soon. Derek didn't even know him. He was just projecting his own behavior onto Steven, and it wasn't fair. "He sent me a ScentBook message the other day. He was asking how I am."

"What a prince. What did you say?"

I shoved my chair back. "This isn't about him." I felt about ten seconds from just walking out. "This is about me. I'm changing too."

"Yeah," he said. "You're changing really fucking fast, and I want to make sure you're not doing it because Jeremy's pushing you, or because you want to be like Steven, or, hell, because you wanna be like me."

"If I wanted to be like you, I'd drink more protein shakes," I said, meanly.

"You could stand to. If you wanna buff up, I'll help. But I meant: I worked my way up to sleeping around. You're just diving in. What is it, four guys in two weeks now? Counting the mystery fox?"

"Yeah. More than in the…" No need to be completely honest. "The past four years."

"Well, that's—that's not the Lonnie I know."

"No, bro," I said. "That is the Lonnie you know, now."

Our eyes locked, and then he shook his head. "I'm just worried that you're kinda cray over the breakup. I seen it happen with guys, and they fuck up their lives. I don't want you to go all, like, epic fail."

I scraped my claws along the napkin in my lap. "Look, if the guys I've been with are any indication, I can see why you'd be worried. If I didn't insist on condoms, nobody would put one on."

That wasn't Derek's big problem, and I knew it, and I think he knew I knew it. He just picked up another meat cube and chewed it up. "Well, it ain't the eighties no more."

"Nor is it the—whatever the fuck the double-zeroes were. I'm not a shy high school cub."

He picked up the last cube of meat and bit it delicately off his fork, lips pulled back from his teeth, and then chewed thoughtfully. "No, I see that. I guess I was wrong."

And maybe it was the new me. Maybe two weeks ago I would've just been quiet and sad and thought, Derek's disappointed in me somehow. But Jeremy's advice was carrying me now, starch in my spine, fire in my eyes. "So…what? Are you friend-dumping me?"

I asked it deliberately starkly like that. His eyes widened and he put his fork down. "Oh, no, bro, I didn't mean—no, it's just—"

"Then what is it?" I pushed my plate to one side and rested my elbows on the table. "You've been acting as weird about this as Jeremy. He acts like he's got money on how many guys I sleep with this week, setting me up at a club, getting me new clothes, taking me to meet his friends…"

Derek's ears swept back when I said "money." He looked down at the table and I sat up straighter. "You know something about Jeremy."

"Uh." He stared down at his rice, like really tried to bore a hole through his plate with his eyes.

"Derek." He still didn't look up. I played another card, which might have been my last. "I know we weren't best bros or anything, but you're about the closest friend I got left. So if there's something I ought to know…"

"I'm not supposed to say," he mumbled.

"Your ears already said it, and Jesus Dog look at the way your whiskers are drooping! What's he doing? Does he really have money on me?" Derek nodded, slowly. "What? Seriously?"

First, I felt obscurely good that Jeremy had bet someone money, real money, that I would be able to sleep with a bunch of guys. It was odd—kind of, now I thought about it, like being a prostitute by proxy—but nobody would ever have bet on me like that a year ago, or even two months ago. I felt sexy and my tail wagged even though I was sort of upset at Derek. I mean, I wouldn't have *not* tried to sleep with these guys if I'd known there was money on it.

Derek rubbed his muzzle. "Sort of," he said.

"So how much is on me?"

"Uh. Dinner at Chez Marchand. So probably like a hundred, hundred-fifty." He made a face. "Jeremy likes wine."

"Whoa." I stared at him, at the crease of dark fur between his eyebrows and the short fur sticking up every which way there. His ears remained splayed out to the side, and his eyes kind of peered up at me. "You bet against me?"

He nodded again, slowly, and rubbed his nose. "Sorry. I didn't mean…I mean, I thought I knew you, and at the Blue Moon, Jeremy was all like, 'The cherry's popped now,' and 'your little wolf will be all over Cottage Hill before you know it,' and we'd both had a couple drinks…" He spread his paws.

I was starting to not feel so good about being the subject of the bet. My tail stilled. "So what was the bet?"

He cleared his throat. "He bet that you'd fuck three guys in the next three weeks. To find your mystery fox. You know, 'cause you just had his jizz smell in your shorts."

"I remember."

"Anyway, I thought, Lonnie'd never go on a 'Jizzin' Quest.'"

"I prefer 'fitting a glass condom,' but go on."

He screwed up his eyes, fur wrinkling between them. "Ouch. That'd hurt. And what if it broke?"

"It's figurative." I waved a paw. "Don't change the subject."

"So we made the bet. We could both help—or not help—but not, y'know, be there when it happened. Jeremy thought you had it in you, and I didn't. I guess he was right."

"Yeah, well." My phone buzzed; I ignored it. I thought about Steven's "are you okay" message, the one I hadn't replied to. I thought about all the nice stuff Jeremy'd done for me, the help he'd given me and the clothes he'd gotten, all not because he liked me, but because he wanted to win a bet.

The night with Porton made more sense now. Maybe he hadn't even been at the party. Maybe Jeremy knew who my mystery fox was, maybe he'd always known, and he'd just set up the three mystery guys so I would definitely sleep with them. Porton was a friend of his; I imagined Jeremy calling him up and saying, "I've got this wolf you can fuck if you just pretend you might've been at a party with him." Porton wasn't really my type otherwise. Hell, he'd barely seemed interested in me even when I was throwing myself at him.

And if he wasn't my type, then what was Cristal? How improbable had that been? Maybe Jeremy knew Cristal, too, and had told him to watch out for the handkerchief, the code that nobody else seemed to know. Both Cristal and Porton had balked at using condoms, but had gone ahead anyway. Would they have done that for some random wolf they'd just met? Or were they paying off favors to a certain black rat?

And had Jeremy known all along that it was Wendell, only saving him for last because then I would stop sleeping around? Or had he just picked three foxes he knew he could get me in bed with?

"Hey," Derek said, reaching across the table. "I'm happy you're doing it, y'know. I don't mind buying Jeremy the dinner."

"Oh, fuck the dinner," I said, louder than I'd intended to.

My ears were back, too. Derek leaned forward. "You're mad."

"Yeah, I'm mad."

"At me?" His ears slid up slowly. "Or at Jeremy?"

"At both of you!" I crumpled my napkin and threw it on the table. "You guys just…you bet on me, like some kind of…like a racing bird or something, just to see what you could make me do. You didn't think about what I needed, or how to help me. You just thought, 'hey, it'll be fun to throw the poor little *ommie,*'" I hurled the word at him, "'out into the jungle and see if he fucks or not.' It's…" I put a paw to my nose. "It's not the kind of thing you do to a friend."

Derek had hunched in on himself while I was talking, all those muscles pulling inward as his muzzle dipped lower and lower, his ears flat. When I finished, he mumbled, "I just wanted to help."

"Yeah, well, you helped all right. Thanks for telling me about the bet. I'm glad I know what's really been going on around here." I felt all jagged edges and tight pressure, and I didn't want to erupt at Derek, but for crying out loud, if he was worried about me having too much sex, he could have *told me,* or introduced me to different people, or done pretty much anything except bet on me and then do *nothing.*

"It's not like that," he said, but he still wouldn't look at me. "I made a mistake. I'm sorry."

So I pushed myself out of the booth. "Yeah, well, I guess maybe I did too." I took two steps and then turned. "By the way, it's 'cray-cray,' not just 'cray.' If you mean 'crazy,' that is." And I walked out.

CHAPTER NINE

When I got home, I threw the phone onto the desk and sat down in my desk chair so quickly that I kinked my tail. I straightened it out and slumped back, clapping my paws over my eyes and muzzle. All the way home my thoughts had spiraled downward faster and faster.

I'd been so proud of how I was meeting people and making friends, and it turned out that it was all staged, that it was all Jeremy's doing to win a bet. All except, presumably, the sex I'd had at the party, and wasn't *that* something to be proud of: so drunk I couldn't even remember the other guy's name or his scent or what his face looked like. Maybe if I got really drunk, next time I could forget the species too, and just remember how thick the cock that pushed into me was.

I should just buy a thick sex toy and shove it up my tail every night. I could complain to it about being lonely, and nobody would have to cash in favors to get me laid. Derek and Jeremy could bet on that for sure.

Of course the rat had set it all up. I don't know why I thought I'd be able to just come down here and become part of this community where everyone talked about sex all the time like it was a barter system.

Mom would be able to tell me that I was going to be fine. She'd say a lot of words that would make me feel better without actually meaning anything. But I couldn't talk to her about what was going on here, not yet. I needed someone whom I could talk to about being gay.

So I pulled up ScentBook on my computer, and the last thing I'd looked at was Steven's message. *Are you okay? Sure looks like you're making a lot of new friends.*

Even broken up, Steven still cared about me. He thought I was making new friends, wanted to know if I was okay. We hadn't worked as a couple, but that was my fault, and now of course I remembered all the times he'd wanted to go out and I made him stay in, the time I'd drunkenly made a pass at one of our friends (as he explained, it didn't matter that I didn't mean anything, it was how it *looked*), the time we'd driven two hours to get to the concert and I forgot the tickets, the time I fucked up in front of his friends (not the time I came on to Brad; the time I made fun of him for how much time he took to prep his fur, which he said made him look vain), the time I fucked up in front of his *family* (I assumed we'd be staying in a room together even though he'd told me his family was still getting used to his orientation)…my dad, the one time he'd met Steven, had said, "He's too good for you," and we'd laughed, but he'd been right.

My fingers started typing, the words just coming out along with choking noises in my throat. I told him I wasn't okay, that I'd made a huge mistake coming to Port City, that everyone here was shallow and only cared about sex, whether getting it themselves or getting other people to do it, that I didn't belong here and I wanted to go back to Freestone. I knew as I was typing that it was pathetic, but I didn't care. Even when I fucked up, Steven always patted me and told me it was okay.

Except that last time. My fingers hesitated, but only a moment. That last time didn't matter, and anyway, who could blame him? We were still friends, we still cared about each other. I read back over what I'd written and didn't see anything that was too pathetic. I wasn't asking him to come back to me or dump Cranston or anything. It was fine. I hit Send.

Then I pulled out my phone, wondering if Steven would send a message or call, and I saw the message that had come in over dinner. It was Taylor, saying that he and Wendell would love to have me over Saturday night.

I guess that's how long Jeremy told them to wait before inviting me over. Like there was any doubt. Well, if it had been just me, they wouldn't give me a second look, but as a favor to Jeremy, I guess they'd suck it up. Maybe literally. Ha ha.

Well, I didn't need to be anyone's pity fuck, not again. I wiped my nose, typed, *sorry i don't think i can*, and sent it.

The really bad part was that before Derek had told me it was all because of a bet, I'd been enjoying myself. I'd been proud of how I'd been forward with Porton, how I'd dressed up and been fashionable with Cristal, how I'd gone with the flow with Geoff and hell, even how I'd handled the mugging. I was still a bit skittish, but it was something that happened in the city, and it had happened to me, and I was alive. But now it turned out that maybe I'd been completely boring to Porton, and the only fashion that had mattered with Cristal had been the handkerchief. Even Geoff probably knew Jeremy and had been told to find me and keep me occupied without getting me off. Why else would you take a guy behind a hedge and rub his cock for fifteen minutes and then just take a picture?

All of the things I thought I'd done well would have come out the same no matter what I did, and the fact that Jeremy'd had to arrange them all just proved how clumsy and lame I was. The only thing I'd managed to do myself was stumble into the wrong part of town and get mugged. The big tiger's paw on my shoulder was the only intimate contact Port City wanted to have with me.

In the middle of blowing my nose, my phone rang. Steven, I thought, but when I grabbed the phone, it was Taylor's number. I thought about just ignoring it. I didn't really want to have a big conversation, and I was mad at Jeremy and myself, not him. But reflex and courtesy made me pick up the phone.

"Sorry, Lonnie," the civet said. "I'm old-school and I like to talk to people. Are you okay?"

"I'm, uh, I'm fine." And then I sniffed loudly.

"You're not fine," Taylor said. "I thought your message seemed a little off, and now you sound…" He paused. "Upset."

"I'm not…" I breathed in. "I'm not upset at you."

"Is it something you'd like to talk about?"

"No." My chest ached. "I don't know."

He spoke patiently. "I can't help feeling it must have something to do with us, since you declined our invitation. Was it just a coincidence?"

"No. I…no. But…"

He listened while I tried to work out the right words to say, and finally he said, "I promise you, if you need someone to talk to who isn't involved with any of this, I'm happy to listen."

Steven wasn't calling me. And Taylor was being patient and sensible. "I don't want to…I mean, I don't need to…It's just Jeremy, I thought…I found out that…"

"Take a breath, wolf. You don't have to get it all out at once."

I did, and organized my thoughts. "What did Jeremy tell you about me?"

"Jeremy? He just said you were new in town and you were available and he thought we'd get along. He said you were open to…" There was a small click, a tap of claw against fang. "Having fun. Sex."

"That's all?"

"That's all. Was that not true? What did you think he told us?"

I breathed in again. "No, it's true, it's…at least, I'm new and available, but…I just found out that…" It was hard to say, and Taylor didn't wait for me to get my thoughts sorted this time.

"Would you like me to come over?"

"Oh, jeez. Oh, no, you don't have to…"

"How far are you from Cottage Hill?"

I wiped my nose again. "Ten minute subway ride, but…"

"Then it's no trouble. I can be there in twenty. Just say the word."

I paced around the room, holding the phone. "Taylor, I really appreciate it, but…I don't know if I'm ready for…"

"Lonnie. Jeremy told me one other thing, just a little bit ago when I called to tell him we were inviting you." He waited, and I didn't say anything. "He said you might be upset at him. Are you?"

"Did he tell you why?"

"No. But do you have anyone else to talk to?"

I didn't want to say no, because it sounded pathetic, but by the time I thought of something else to say, my silence had spoken for me. "All right. I'm coming over."

"But…"

"No sex, Lonnie. Just listening. Promise."

"That's not what I—" But it had been what I was thinking. I felt a wash of relief go through me. "You're sure it's no trouble?"

"None at all. I'm delighted to help."

So I gave him my address, and he made me promise to drink water even though I told him I hadn't been drinking, and then he hung up. I slid the phone into my pocket and went about straightening up the apartment. It really helped to have something to do with my paws, a goal that I could work on while just shutting down my mind. I got the clothes off the floor, cleaned up the takeout boxes, and took the garbage down to the chute. I even got the little hand vacuum out and vacuumed up the carpet. *I* did this, I thought, taking a drink of water. I cleaned up the apartment for a friend, someone who wanted to come see me. And when the door buzzer sounded, I jumped to answer it.

Taylor stepped into the apartment wearing a big smile on both his muzzle and his black-masked eyes and extended his arms, first thing. He wasn't tall, didn't have red fur, and didn't have handsome black ears or a big bushy tail, and that was disappointing—but only for a second. So I stepped into the hug, and it felt pretty good and I held it maybe longer than he expected me to, but he didn't complain. I inhaled his sharp vivverid musk as I released him, and I was proud of myself for not getting emotional in the hug. "Nice place," he said as he placed a small paper bag in my paw. "I like the art. Those are places you've been?"

"Uh, some of them." I pointed. "I went to Devil Canyon in college for a field trip, and that one I took when I was in Gallia skiing. They're just interesting geological formations."

"They're also lovely pictures." He spread his arms. "This is spacious for a Port City apartment. There's somewhere I can stand where I can't touch a wall."

I laughed a little, which felt good. Then I caught an aroma from the bag he'd given me and brought it to my nose. Cinnamon wafted out, along with something floral and light. Rosewater, maybe? "What is this?"

"Oh," Taylor said, "I got you a little treat. Those are candies from a little Alexandrian shop a block from here. The store owners, Ethiopian wolves, are gay…came here to escape persecution. I've marched with them for years. These are candies for wolves." He waved fingers at them. "Special spice combination. You're supposed to sniff them three times and then lick and then eat."

"Wow." I teased the bag open and caught another spice: saffron. Two one-inch cubes sat on a wax sheet in the paper bag. "One for you?"

"If you would like to share. I know I can't appreciate them the way you can, but they're still delicious."

So a minute or two later we were sitting on my futon, each with a glass of water, the exotic candies still a sweet memory in my nose and tongue. Taylor rested his paws on his knees, looked seriously at me, and said, "Tell me about it."

So I took a breath and started from the beginning, how I'd had sex at McMinaver's, and then I remembered that that wasn't the beginning, so I went back and told him how Steven had dumped me. He listened, sometimes lifting a claw to tap one of his fangs, as I told him about Jeremy helping me try to figure out who the fox had been, and how that was all a cover for just trying to win a bet with Derek. My jagged edges had smoothed by the time I got to Porton and Cristal, hesitating over the amount of sexual detail to put in, but he didn't press, just accepted a short "I took him in my muzzle" and "I made him put on a condom." Then I came to the dinner with him and Wendell, and I went quiet.

"You think Wendell might have been the fox at the party." Taylor had set his drink down and folded his paws together.

"I don't know what to think." Only then did it really click with me that I was telling Taylor that his husband might have cheated on him with me. "He didn't react at all when I mentioned the party. I don't even know if he was there. I mean, Jeremy said…"

"He was." Taylor rubbed his muzzle. "He likes those parties more than I do."

"I'm sure he didn't cheat on you," I said.

The civet raised his eyebrows, with a half-smile. "Are you?" He met my eyes and I didn't know what to say to him. I forgot for a moment the stress I was under and felt his pain. "Unless you actually get the scent, you won't know, will you?"

"No."

He picked up his water and took a drink. "Or unless you let me sniff it."

I took a drink myself to cover up my mind's racing. I could give Taylor the boxers and he could settle the whole thing right now. But if it had been Wendell, then I didn't want to be the one who'd told on him. "I, uh," I lowered my ears. "I tossed them in the laundry downstairs when I got home. I was so mad at Jeremy I just wanted to be done with it."

"Ah." He sat back and traced claws along his pants, and then, when I didn't say anything, reached over to pat mine. "It wouldn't break up our marriage. We've been together years and we've both done things we've hidden from the other at first."

I didn't know what to say, so I just nodded, and Taylor smiled and went on. "But I don't want to make this about us. Was there anything else you wanted to say?"

"You've been part of this community a long time," I said, and he nodded. "Can you tell me—"

My phone rang. I fished it out of my pocket, mumbling apologies, and my heart stopped when I saw the name and picture on it. Steven was calling me. He really was calling me back.

I lifted my muzzle to Taylor. "Sorry, I…"

He got up from the couch with a knowing smile. But I didn't pick up the call. What was I going to say to Steven? I could tell him what I'd just told Taylor, and he would tell me how disgusting everyone in Port City was. I couldn't ask him what I wanted to ask Taylor; besides which, I felt bad for Taylor and I didn't want to just send him away after putting doubts in his head. Steven? I didn't even know if I wanted to tell him anything. But I couldn't just let it go to voicemail, not after that message I'd sent. So I held up my paw and said to Taylor, "Don't go."

He turned and tilted his head, watching me, his eyes bright in his black mask.

I took a breath and picked up the call. "Hi, Steven." I still didn't know what I was going to say.

"Hi, Lonnie. You sounded bad."

His voice. This wasn't the Steven on ScentBook or the Steven in my memory. This was his actual voice, the Steven Derek had been talking about, the Steven who had looked so uncomfortable as he'd said, "*This is really hard for me…*" My whole ScentBook message ran back through my head, only now I was looking at it the way Steven must have seen it.

"Thanks for calling," I said. "I'm sorry for sending that stupid message. I'm in the middle of something right now, can I call you back?"

He was quiet for a second, and then he said, "Yeah, okay." He didn't even argue, didn't press to make sure I was all right. After a pause, he did say, "You sure?"

"Yeah," I lied. "Thanks."

I set the phone down and put my paws in my lap. "Sorry about that."

Taylor sat back down, a little closer to me, a wide grin on his muzzle. The light touches of grey on his ears and mask were only visible this close; apart from that, I wouldn't be able to tell he was old. Not *old*, but older than me. I'd thought Taylor and Wendell both moved with the slow grace of age, but maybe Taylor just matched his movements to his husband's. He still radiated the same experienced assurance, but his movements were quicker here than they'd been Wednesday night. "That was…the ex-boyfriend?"

"Uh-huh. I sent him a…" I exhaled. "A dumb emotional message. God, it was just an hour ago."

Taylor patted my paw. "You're young. You'll do that."

"All my friends are young." I laughed a little shakily. "None of them did anything like this."

He raised an eyebrow. "Really?"

"Yeah. I mean, when Steven and I were together, we had a dozen friends, and they broke up and got together and broke up again and there weren't any big meltdowns. I mean, that I ever heard of."

Taylor was quiet, but his eyes didn't leave mine. He took my paw in his little one and said, "I hope I'm not out of line by asking, but are you still close to any of them?"

"I…well, no." I frowned. "I mean, we're ScentBook friends still. Bret and Mitch liked my post about moving here. Jordan said, 'Way to go.' "

"All right, I know ScentBook is all well and good, but…" He hesitated. "I'm just saying that if you didn't hear about anyone doing anything stupid with their relationship, then they just didn't tell you about it. So I deduced that most of those people weren't real close friends." He watched my eyes. "I'm sorry."

"No." I looked back and then nodded. "You're right. I mean, they're still watching me on ScentBook, but that's easy. None of them really make any effort." My tail uncurled, and I relaxed into the couch. "You mean what I did is normal? Did you ever do that?"

He squeezed my paw as his eyes sparkled. "Oh, wolf. You remember that eighties movie where the guy stands outside his girl's window with a boombox? I actually for real swear to you that I did that."

"Really?" My emo message to Steven didn't seem so bad. "What happened?"

He released my paw and cleared his throat. "Well, the object of my affection was out getting affection from his new boyfriend, and his father sprayed me with a garden hose."

"Oh god." I put a paw to my nose.

The civet waved, his mask creasing up in a smile. "It was longer ago than you've been alive, and now I have a funny story to tell."

"I bet it wasn't funny at the time."

"Well, no," he conceded. "But comedy is just tragedy plus time, and nobody was hurt. Except my boombox, and honestly, good riddance."

"What happened to the ex-boyfriend?"

The smile faltered, and his little round ears lay back. "He died a while back. We didn't stay close; I heard through one of the groups I work with."

"Oh, I'm sorry."

We were quiet for a moment, and then he said, "So this is why you don't think you can come over Saturday?"

I thought back, lowered my muzzle, and stared at my paws. "I don't know now."

"Let me just say a thing or two, if I may?" I nodded, and Taylor drew his legs up on the couch and sat cross-legged. "Okay. Like I said, Jeremy only told us you were sweet and that he thought you'd hit it off with us. Wendell and I talked about it after dinner and we decided he was right. That's why we invited you back Saturday—the only reason." He rested his bluntly pointed muzzle in his paw, leaning his elbow on the back of the futon. "We'd still like you to come over, just to get to know you better. No pressure for anything else. If you want to wait until next week or the week after, that's fine. But whatever you decide, I hope you'll find some friends here."

"I just don't know if I belong here," I said because it was dramatic, and Taylor gave me a look. "All right, I'm probably overreacting to this."

"A little." He curled his tail around into his lap. "It wasn't a very nice thing to do, I agree. But it doesn't seem like it was very harmful overall. I mean, unless I'm misreading, he left the option of sex up to you in all the cases. He might've stacked the deck a little, but you were never coerced into anything. Were you?"

"No." I thought back. "No, it was always up to me."

"In fact, you almost didn't do it with Cristal because of the condom."

"That's right." I held up a finger. "And I got to feel up a mink. I'm…I'm pretty sure I did that on my own."

"Oh, good for you." He reached out and pushed my shoulder gently. "So what was the problem?"

Our eyes met and I breathed shakily. "The whole thing where I wasn't sure if I could get by, if these people were really my friends."

"Lonnie," he said, "I always hated when older people tried to force their wisdom on me, but as I get older I find myself doing it more and more, and so here comes a little bit that I hope will help. In my fifty-some years I have still not found a way to tell whether someone is your friend, really your friend, except for time. And you've been here less than three months. You're going to meet a lot of people, and many of them will not be your friends. But there's no shortcut to finding out which ones those are."

"I, uh." I rubbed a paw along my thigh and looked up at him. "I think…I'm pretty sure I have at least one friend."

His bright smile showed the points of his fangs. "I'm glad. I'd hate for you to give up on Jeremy so quickly."

I had to laugh again. "Him, too. Hey, thanks for coming over." My smile came more easily than I would've thought. "I'll let you know about Saturday. But…"

He read my expression. "But what if Wendell was your fox?"

"Yeah."

Taylor took my paw and held it. "If you'd rather not go through with it, that's okay," he said. "But if you do, then don't worry about what it means to us. I'd rather know than not."

He looked serious, and I curled my fingers around his warm black paw, smaller than Steven's, way smaller than Derek's. "You sure?" I asked.

"You've got my number," he said. We both stood, and he hugged me good-bye.

I had another call to make, too, and one I felt better equipped to make now. I took my phone out, but the first thing I saw was the most recent call—the one from Steven. His name and the picture I'd used as his contact photo shone up out of the phone at me. Behind his red-furred muzzle and large black ears, the sky and sea were a bright blue. We'd been on the ferry coming back from a romantic weekend on Kanset Island. Our hotel had lost power during a storm and we'd had sex, then lain awake talking, and had sex again. It was my favorite weekend with Steven ever. He'd put his arm around me there on the ferry in public and curled his long fox's tail around mine and told me how happy he was.

Six months later, he dumped me.

I cleared the phone and called Derek. "Hey," I said, and then took a breath. "Sorry."

We talked for a little while. I didn't tell him Taylor had come over. After that, I called Jeremy to let him know that I wasn't too upset with him but that I'd see him and Derek Sunday morning at The Morning After. And then I went to bed.

CHAPTER TEN

There must have been a party somewhere Saturday night, because The Morning After assaulted me with a fog of scents and noise as soon as I walked in. Gilliam sat in a corner toward the front with Martique and Victor and an arctic fox; the three I knew waved at me and the arctic fox looked up with a smile. Porton sat under the big pink rooster across from a short black wolf, and as I walked past him, our eyes met with a short, "Hey." The black wolf asked who I was, and Porton said, "That's Lonnie. You don't know him?"

I squeezed behind a table of Derek's muscle buddies, one of whom called out, "Hey, Lonnie! You ever find that mystery guy?"

"Nope." I grinned at him and went on, ears perked back to listen to him explain my ScentBook post to the rest of the table. I figured I'd have a couple new followers by the time I got home.

Jeremy and Derek were talking by the window, Jeremy in a red fishnet vest and loose pink pants, his legs crossed; Derek in a white tank top and jeans. Even in this eclectic crowd, they looked a spectacularly odd couple, and they were only together this morning because of me, because they both cared about me. It helped to think of it that way.

They each had a mimosa and had one waiting for me. I slid into the chair facing the window, curled my tail around the back support, and tipped the flute to my lips.

"We gambled that you didn't get too drunk last night," Jeremy said.

"We didn't *actually* bet," Derek said earnestly.

I perked my ears to show them I was feeling good. "You're right. I'm fine, no hangover. This is pretty good."

"They use champagne that's cheaper than orange juice," Jeremy said, "but the juice cuts it enough that you don't really notice."

"Tastes fine to me." They watched me as I sipped slowly. "So," I said, "where was the party last night?"

The rat and wolf exchanged looks, and Jeremy answered. "The Twenty-One. DJ Loop was there."

"Ah." I set down my glass and smiled. "Good dancing?"

"I'm sorry about not telling you about the bet," Derek burst out.

"I know. You told me on the phone."

"Yeah, but you haven't called in three days and I'm still sorry." His arms bunched up as his paws clenched around a napkin.

"I overreacted," I said. I lay my elbows on the table and rested my muzzle on my paws. "I'm still…" Sheesh. I'd practiced this speech and everything and still I couldn't quite say it right the first time. "This whole community here is cool and I like it, but it's taking me a while to figure out that I belong. It just made me feel like I was an outsider, and so I kinda went a little nuts over it."

Derek eyed me. "You didn't call the asshole, did you?"

"Uh." I folded my ears back. "I didn't *call* him…"

"Lonnie," Derek sighed.

"No, it's cool, I kinda, uh, I whined at him on ScentBook and he called me but Taylor came over and so I didn't talk to Steven."

"Taylor?" Jeremy leaned forward. "He didn't tell me that."

I nodded. "I know. I asked him not to. He helped a lot. He pointed out that what you guys did wasn't necessarily hurtful, but he understood why I felt like I did."

"We weren't thinking it would hurt you, not at all," Jeremy said, and Derek shook his head in agreement. "Derek wanted to tell you, in fact. I thought if you knew about the bet, you would pick Derek to win because it was the easier, safer thing."

"And then I wouldn't even try to sleep with anyone?" He nodded. "Interesting. I don't know what I would've done." Rolling the possibility over in my mind, there was still the uncomfortable sensation of being a show bird. But I also liked the idea that Jeremy saw potential in me that nobody else had, even if that potential was to be slutty. Well, no. To be adventurous, to be part of his circle.

The black rat cleared his throat and took a sip of his mimosa. "So what did you do?"

Derek elbowed him, which made the rat clutch his arm dramatically. "Let him tell us in his own time, you said."

"He was just speculating on what he would have done if he'd known about the bet. Well, he knew Saturday night, so I'm just following the conversation along its logical progression to ask him what he *did* do."

I raised my eyebrows and waited a moment for an eruption of laughs and hoots behind me (from Derek's muscle buddies, I was sure) to die down. "So you know I went over there Saturday night."

"I do now." Jeremy smiled broadly at me, folding his paws with their red-painted claws together.

I shook my head and gave Derek a look, pointing at Jeremy. "He's as tricky as a coyote."

"We rats have our secrets too. So was Wendell the one?"

"The one what?" The orange juice and champagne taste was going stale on my tongue, so I took another drink.

Derek glared at me. "The one who fucked you at the party, you cocktease."

He said it loud enough to still the conversations immediately around us. I flattened my ears and stared down at the menu. "Did you guys order food yet?"

Everyone at the nearby tables who'd looked up at me looked away again quickly when I turned to signal the waiter. The groundhog in the vest took a little while to come over, and then I pretended to take a while to decide what I wanted. When he'd scribbled down our orders and gone again, both Jeremy and Derek looked satisfyingly impatient.

"All right," I said. "Now, what were you asking?"

"Whether you know how to get orange juice and champagne out of your fur," Derek growled. "We were shitty about the bet, but you're milkin' it now."

"He's entitled," Jeremy said, though I could see his pink tail twitching.

I grinned, and because I wanted to get to the next part, I said, "No, he's not the one."

Derek sagged in his chair. "You did sleep with him."

I widened my eyes. "I didn't say that."

Jeremy tapped one finger against his muzzle as Derek straightened. "Are you going to tell us?"

My tail wagged. "Nope."

"He slept with them," Jeremy said.

Derek grinned at me. "I dunno. You didn't see him Thursday."

"I know Taylor." Jeremy gave me a wink.

"Okay," Derek said, "But how will you prove it?"

Jeremy opened his muzzle, and I cut off what I knew he was going to say. "Taylor and Wendell promised not to tell."

They looked at each other. "So the bet's off?"

"Not really." I held up a finger. "I decided that you both have to take *me* out to dinner. At…that place, whatever it was."

The rat and wolf stared at me, then both chuckled. "I guess that's fair," Derek said.

"And rather poetically just."

"It was Wendell's idea," I admitted.

"You told them about the bet?"

I nodded. "And about the mystery fox. Wendell helped me…make sure."

Derek shook his head, and Jeremy brushed his whiskers back. For a moment, I was worried that I'd said too much; Wendell and Taylor had cautioned me to keep it simple. But the rat only asked, "How did Taylor take it?"

"He was upset that Wendell went to the party, but he knew about that already. They were both curious about what fox it could've been, but they said there were a bunch there, and Taylor pointed out that all of your eleven or whatever might have reasons for not posting that you didn't know about." The whole conversation with them had taken all of fifteen minutes. Taylor had asked if I wanted to go through the list and see if any details clicked with me, but I said that all I really had to go on was the scent.

"So you going on with this Jizzin' Quest?" Derek asked.

"Nah." I exhaled. "It was kinda dumb anyway. If the guy doesn't want me to find him, then I won't. I tossed the boxers in the laundry." This had not been true when I said it to Taylor Thursday night, but it was now. "I'm just going to spend more time down here and get to know more people."

"I approve of that plan," Jeremy said.

"Yeah." Derek gulped down the rest of his mimosa. "If you want a membership at the gym, just lemme know."

"Thanks. I might do that." Taylor and Wendell had mentioned that they both worked out and recommended I get into the habit. Also, Taylor had said, there were lots of cute guys at the gym who weren't bodybuilders.

"And there's a concert at the Troc next week," Jeremy said.

"Oh! O'Shea's has a trivia night." Derek squeezed my shoulder. "You'd be great at that."

Our food arrived then, and we tucked in. Partway through eating, another friend of Jeremy's came over and we told him he could join us, so I met Koty the talkative stallion. Two of Koty's friends came over about twenty minutes later, and we pulled a nearby table over and all six crammed around it, and that's how I got invited to watch an FBA game the following Thursday night. "I don't really know much about basketball," I said, "but I'll hang out and learn."

The newcomers ordered food and were eating and talking after the three of us had finished, and Koty was telling Jeremy about this new album he'd heard. Derek leaned over to me and said quietly, "I can teach you a bit about basketball if you wanna bone up before you go over. I mean, brush up." His ears flicked back and he grinned bashfully.

"Maybe." I smiled. "Basketball was Steven's thing. He played in prep and he and his friends followed the FBA. I never really got into it with him, but maybe with a different group..."

"Ah." Derek glanced at the stallion, who was singing part of one of the songs for Jeremy. "None of them's a fox."

"I'm not off foxes," I said. "Not hardly. But I think I might be over Steven." I hadn't called him back after Thursday night, and he hadn't called back either. I thought he was probably relieved to be rid of me. I felt the same.

"About fucking time," Derek said, and he wrapped a powerful arm around me. "Let's drink to that."

"What are we drinking to?" Koty perked his little ears up, and his friends quieted too.

Derek picked up his glass. "To Lonnie getting over his shitbag of an ex."

"Awesome!" "Yeah!" Broad smiles shone my way as everyone picked up a glass. Jeremy's smile curved up and up into his black cheekruffs, showing his fangs, and his eyes met mine with warm approval.

Derek kept his arm around my shoulder and lifted his champagne flute. "To Lonnie, and fuck Steven."

"Fuck Steven!" the table chorused.

"That's someone else's job now," I said, and everyone laughed as they clinked glasses. I clinked with them, held the glass to my nose until the sweet orange and sharp champagne filled my nostrils, and drank.

Epilogue: One Month Later

"First to the shower," Taylor sang, and leapt from the bed, all spots and matted fur, dashing to the bathroom. The door slammed shut.

Wendell slid carefully out of me and peeled the condom off his still-hard cock. He reached over the edge of the bed to drop it in the trash while I flipped over onto my back and lay there on the towel. His paw caressed my stomach, and I closed my eyes. "Have a good time?" he asked softly.

I cracked one eye open and then reached a paw down to my erection, lifting it and smearing my jizz on one finger so it dripped onto my stomach. "What's it look like?"

He chuckled. "Well, there's a good time and then there's a *good* good time."

"Yeah," I said. "It was good. How about you two?"

"We're still having fun." He looked great naked, creamy white and autumn reds and oranges and browns, muscles and a soft layer of fat around his middle, but not too much. Pretty hazel eyes and grey at the tips of his black ears and he did not remind me of Steven, no, not even in the throes of sex when his knot stretched me and then filled me. I had too many memories now, too much buffer between me and my ex, so I appreciated Wendell for Wendell.

I shifted a leg to trap his tail beneath it, and he made it squirm against the towel, while moving his claws to my side to tickle me in revenge. "Hey," I yelped, "not fair!"

He chuckled and kept tickling until I said, "I give!" and lifted my knee, freeing his tail.

"You're cute when you're ticklish like that." He slid his paw below my leg, probed at the warmth his cock had so recently vacated, rubbing around and gently into me. "You're used to fox knots, I guess. Not sore?"

"Nnf," I said, and turned my head to look at him. In the other room, the shower started running. This was the moment to say something, but he was looking at me casually, with an affectionate smile. I couldn't do it.

And then Taylor started singing, "Walking on Sunshine," and I took a breath. "No. I wasn't after the party, either."

He froze, his finger resting where it was, even his tail going still. "With that fox?" he said carefully.

"I recognized your scent." I lowered my voice, even though Taylor would never have heard us. "And you recognized me, I think—I think."

Slowly, he nodded, and now withdrew his paw, trailing it along my hip. "I wasn't a hundred percent sure. I was drunk, too, but how many wolves can there be who slept with foxes they didn't remember? When did you know?"

"I, uh." I folded my ears back. It was one thing to go around searching for the matching scent of the come of some mystery fox. It was another to look in the eyes of a guy you've seen for dinner five or six times, seen naked three times and just had inside you for the first time, a guy you've developed a relationship with, and confess to him that all this time you've known a secret he thought was safe.

But I'd spent a month coming to terms with being friends to these two, all the while knowing that I was part of that secret, that I was "the other guy." I'd never cheated on Steven, but if I had, I don't think he would have forgiven me. I was pretty sure that Taylor would forgive Wendell, and that, like sharing their bed, was an idea I was getting used to. Relationships were more complicated and varied than I'd ever known, and as afraid as I was of making a misstep, I was even more afraid of not taking an essential step.

"What?" He pressed a paw through my stomach fur. "I thought I was careful."

I reached down and gave his cock a squeeze. "You left a little scent on my fur. Before you put the condom on."

The squeeze got him to exhale through his nostrils. He let the tip of his tongue hang out of the front of his sharp muzzle. "I do get leaky sometimes. Wow. So why didn't you say anything before now?"

I cocked an ear to the bathroom. Shower and singing both continued. "I would've told you right away, if I didn't want to see you again. But I like you guys. And I wanted to see if there was a way to do it without messing everything up. Kinda selfish, I guess."

Wendell's eyes softened and slid away. He lifted his paw and teased a claw through the stickiness on my stomach. "Then why not just keep it quiet? Never let on that you knew?"

Believe me, I'd considered that possibility too. "When he came over to talk me off the ledge, Taylor said something that stuck with me. He said that you don't know who your friends are without time. Well, it's been over a month now, and I want to be a good friend to both of you." This was the part I had been dreading, the reason I hadn't confronted

Wendell before this—that, plus Taylor didn't always shower first. "You've got to tell him."

"Do I?" He sighed as I started to speak, and held up a paw. "I suppose I do. It won't be the first confession between us, and maybe what's come out of it will make it easier."

I lifted a finger still sticky with my come and said, "Maybe don't use that exact phrasing."

He rolled his eyes. "You need to spend less time with Jeremy. Or at least stop picking up his conversational habits."

"I won't do the first, but I'll try for the second." I licked my finger. "So Taylor's cheated on you, too?"

He remained silent for a moment, and swiveled an ear toward the bathroom. "I can go into it in more detail sometime. Meet you for lunch or something. I can't recap sixteen years in three minutes. I guess the easiest way to say it is that there are grey areas. We're not completely closed—as you've seen—but there are rules around what we can do, and they've evolved over the years. I probably—" He sighed. "Definitely didn't follow the rules when I slept with you at the party."

"Why did you?" I know, I know. I wanted him to say I was irresistible and cute. But I was also just curious and trying to get to know him better.

He chuckled. "I was a little mad that he hadn't come to the party, to be honest. It wasn't just that, of course, it was…well, every argument you have in a relationship is really all the previous arguments rolled up into one. I was mad at him, was the point. And I was a little drunk. But I was careful, like I said." His claw traced patterns in my stomach that came to the edge of tickling without actually making me giggle. It felt a lot like foreplay, if the air weren't already thick with the smell of sex. "I wasn't really looking, but when a cute wolf who didn't know me started flirting with me, well…I was dressed down, and I used a condom. And I didn't tell you my name."

I sat up on my elbows, fast enough that he pulled his paw back, startled. "You didn't *tell* me your name!"

"I just said that." His ears splayed, and he squinted at me.

"No, I know." I lay back and closed my eyes and laughed, and the more I laughed, the more I felt like laughing.

Wendell poked a dark brown paw at my stomach, which just made me giggle more. "What?"

"Oh god," I gasped. "I just felt so bad because I couldn't remember your name, and I went to all this trouble to find out who you are, and it turns out you didn't even tell me and you didn't even *want* me to find you."

"Don't think that." He spread his paw and pressed it down, warm and slick on my stomach fur, dark against my creamy ivory. "I'm glad you sought us out. Taylor and I have had fun with thirds in the past, and you're definitely one of the sexiest."

"You don't have to lie," I said. "I already like you."

"Well, it could be that you're the first one who's half our age."

I laughed again just as the shower stopped. My tail wagged against the bed. "You want to shower next? Then you and Taylor can spend time together clean."

"Maybe that'd be better." He leaned down and touched his nose to mine. "Thank you," he said. "For all of that. I promise I'll tell him sometime soon, and then afterwards we'll sit down with you, too."

"And thank you." I reached down lazily and dabbed a bit of the stickiness from the tip of his cock. Holding my finger at my nose, I inhaled. "Won't forget this smell now."

He shook his head and squeezed my sheath. "Nor my name, I hope."

"Nope." I smiled up at him as he got up from the bed. He reached down to ruffle my ears and then turned toward the bathroom.

I craned my neck to watch Wendell walk away, past the chair with my Charles Perrault mauve shirt and starburst-studded tie draped over it. His butt and cute red tail swung from side to side, then I saw his slender muzzle in profile as he turned the corner to the bathroom and disappeared from sight.

Alone, I savored the warmth, the feeling of detached relaxation. The smile remained stretched across my muzzle as I lay back in this bed into which I'd been invited, one paw in the sticky mess on my stomach, a pleasant slippery warmth under my tail. Murmurs of conversation came from the next room, and I lifted my fox-scented finger to my nose. I took a slow breath in and then closed my eyes and let it go.

ABOUT THE AUTHOR

Kyell Gold began writing furry fiction a long, long time ago. In the early days of the 21st century, he got up the courage to write some gay furry romance, first publishing his story "The Prisoner's Release" in Sofawolf Press's adult magazine **Heat**. He has since won twelve Ursa Major awards for his stories and novels, and his acclaimed novel *Out of Position* co-won the Rainbow Award for Best Gay Novel of 2009. His novel "Green Fairy" was nominated for inclusion in the ALA's "Over the Rainbow" list for 2012.

He was not born in California, but now considers it his home. He loves to travel and dine out with his partner of many years, Kit Silver, and can be seen at furry conventions in California, around the country, and abroad. More information about him and his books is available at *http://www.kyellgold.com.*

ABOUT THE ARTIST

Teagan Gavet is a professional illustrator, graphic novelist, and freelance rambler. Find more at:
http://www.teagangavet.com
http://www.furaffinity.net/user/blackteagan

ABOUT CUPCAKES

Cupcakes are novellas, with more substance than short stories, though not as long as novels. The Cupcakes line was developed for FurPlanet by foozzzball, Kyell Gold, and Rikoshi as a reaction to their desire to tell novella-length stories and the lack of publishing opportunities for novellas.

Previous Cupcakes have been nominated four times for Ursa Major awards, winning twice, and three times for Coyotl Awards, winning once.

ABOUT THE PUBLISHER

FurPlanet publishes original works of furry fiction. You can explore their selection at *http://www.furplanet.com*.

CPSIA information can be obtained
at www.ICGtesting.com
Printed in the USA
FFOW03n2021011215
19119FF

9 781614 501978